A Seaside Bookshop Christmas

Jennifer Faye

Lazy Dazy Press

CONTENTS

About this book...

Twelve days before Christmas, the forecast is calling for snow with a hundred percent chance of love as the owner of the Seaside Bookshop risks everything, including her heart.

Christmas returns to Bluestar Island in this heartwarming page-turner. While the small town's holiday calendar is filled with festive events, the friendships of Bluestar's residents are put to the test. Melinda Coleman, owner of the Seaside Bookshop, finds herself making a deal with the town curmudgeon that could cost her everything. While furniture maker Liam Turner is suddenly a full-time single father, he's in over his head with an active three-year-old. It will take these two friends helping each other to keep their lives from imploding, and in the process, they find the most precious gift of all—love.

Includes a holiday recipe for Santa's Mitten cookies!

Bluestar Island series:
Book 1 – Love Blooms (Hannah & Ethan)
Book 2 – Harvest Dance (Aster & Sam)

PROLOGUE

June, Bluestar Island

IT WAS A BEAUTIFUL summer evening.

Melinda Coleman locked up the Seaside Bookshop. She dropped her keys into her purse before strolling through town. A yawn snuck up on her. It had been a long day.

She'd worked late in order to get a new shipment of books up on the shelves, including a bestselling romance novel, which readers had been stopping by the shop daily in hopes of getting a copy. Tomorrow would be the day they would get to read the latest installment in the ongoing series.

She reached for her phone and dialed her father's number. It rang and rang before switching to his voicemail. "Hey, Dad, I was just calling to check in. I haven't heard from you in a couple of days. You must be busy at work. Give me a call when you get this, and we'll get together for lunch or dinner. Either works for me. Talk to you later."

She disconnected the call and slipped her phone back into her purse. With both of them working, it was difficult to find time to get together for a meal. When one was available the other was working.

Not in the mood to go straight home, she strolled toward the beach. Today was Bluestar's Concert on the Beach. The country music was upbeat and loud enough to hear the lyrics word-by-word even from a distance. The closer she got to the event, the more congested the park got. She had been hoping with it being later in the evening, the crowd would have started to dwindle. That didn't appear to be the case. And she didn't like crowds.

With a sigh, she turned toward her apartment. She was a bit tired. She'd go home and have some leftovers before calling it a night. Then, she heard the wail of a siren. That wasn't good and not a common occurrence on the island. She wondered if it might have something to do with the concert. Maybe the partying had gotten out of control.

Five minutes later, she was almost to her apartment when her phone rang. She grabbed it from her purse. The caller ID showed it was her friend Sara Chen.

She pressed the phone to her ear. "Hey, Sara. What's going on?"

"Melinda, it's your father."

Immediately, her chest tightened. *No, no. Don't let anything have happened to him.* "Wha—what is it?"

"He's collapsed. They think it's his heart."

The air hitched in her lungs. In that moment, the bottom completely fell out of her world. This was her worst nightmare come to life.

She wasn't sure if it was shock or what, but her body just sort of went numb. She stood there on the sidewalk for a moment, not sure what she should do next—where she should go—what she should say. Everything in her world had come to a screeching halt.

"Melinda? Did you hear me?" Her friend's voice startled her out of her shocked stupor. "They got his heart started again."

"Whe... Where are you?"

"At the inn."

Her father worked at the Brass Anchor Inn. He'd worked there her entire life. After her mother died, she'd spent a lot of time running around the place while her father worked. It was like a home away from home for her.

"I'm coming." Her own voice sounded distant to her ears.

"Melinda don't. They just loaded him in the ambulance. They're taking him to the medical center. Meet him there."

She mumbled something into the phone. When she went to disconnect the call, she fumbled and dropped the phone. It hit the sidewalk with a thud. She didn't move. Her thoughts were scattered and chaotic.

"Melinda, is everything all right?"

Melinda turned to find Birdie Neill studying her with a worried look on her face. "No. Nothing is right."

Birdie held out something. "Here is your phone."

"Oh, yes. Thank you."

"Would you like to come back to my place? We could have some tea. I find that tea helps calm me down."

Melinda shook her head. "I have to go. He needs me."

She rushed toward the Bluestar Medical Center. Something dripped onto her hand. Was it raining? She glanced up to find the moon shining bright. It wasn't rain. And then she realized they were tears dripping down her face. She continued briskly walking as she swiped at her face.

How was it possible that her father had a heart attack? He was always out walking. And then she realized she had no idea what he ate because she'd been so absorbed with the bookshop. And her father did have a soft spot for meat-lovers pizza. The more meat, the better. She inwardly groaned. She should have paid more attention—been there more. If he lived through this, she would make sure he ate right and got lots of exercise.

He just had to be all right.

At last she reached the Medical Center. She ran up to the desk. "My father was brought in. His name..." She drew an utter blank. Her hands tremored as she waved them around, trying to gather her galloping thoughts. "It's, uh, Harvey. Harvey Coleman."

The older woman behind the counter, with her dark hair neatly pulled up into a bun, nodded her head. "Oh, yes. They are working on him now. If you'll just have a seat over there, someone will be out to speak with you."

Melinda didn't want to sit down. She didn't think it was possible for her to sit still at this point. She was too worked up. "Can I see him? Please."

The poised woman's gaze moved to the computer monitor and then back at her. "I'm sorry. That's not possible at this moment. I'm very sorry."

This couldn't be happening. She felt so helpless. "But I need to know how he is."

"I understand. I wish I had more information."

That wasn't good enough. Melinda shifted her weight from one leg to the other and then back again. Didn't they understand? She was going out of her mind here. They had to tell her something other than to sit down and wait.

And then she latched onto what was scaring her the most. It was the one thing she didn't want to vocalize because putting it out there in the universe was like tempting fate. And yet she couldn't just take a seat in one of the blue plastic chairs—sitting there wondering about her father's condition would drive her mad.

As unshed tears blurred her vision, she blinked repeatedly. "Is... Is he alive?"

She hated that she had to utter those words. Her father still had so much life in him. He was only in his sixties. She'd planned to have him in her life for at least another thirty years. She was much too young to become an orphan. The tears splashed onto her cheeks.

Sympathy shone in the woman's kind eyes. She reached out and patted Melinda's hand. "I'll go see what I can learn. Just have a seat in the waiting area, and I'll be right back."

"Thank you."

Not caring that she must look a mess with tears and makeup streaking down her face, Melinda made her way to the waiting area, which had a handful of people, either waiting to be seen by a doctor or waiting for a loved one.

She wasn't up to making small talk. Her sole focus was on her father. Her friend's words repeated in her mind: *They got his heart started again.* This was so bad. And there was absolutely nothing she could do to help him.

She dropped down onto one of the chairs. With her elbows on her knees, she rested her face in her palms. *Please let him be all right.* She said a prayer. She needed God to hear her.She would make a deal. She would do whatever it took for her father to be better.

It was impossible to get comfortable on the hard plastic chair. She stood and began to pace around the waiting area. Her mind was full of frantic, jumbled thoughts. She felt as though this was a case of déjà vu. And not in a good way.

She sat in this very waiting room as a young child as her mother fought for her life when an undiagnosed aneurysm had burst. The waiting and wondering had been horrific. In the end, her mother hadn't made it.

Now that she was older, she'd often wondered if her mother might have lived if instead of a medical center, Bluestar had a full-fledged hospital. The population had grown a lot since she was a kid, and surely it could support a bigger facility instead of people being transported to the mainland for more advanced care.

The automatic glass door at the entrance swished open. A familiar face entered the waiting area: Kent Turner, Sara's boyfriend. What was he doing here? Maybe he knew something about her father.

He approached her. "How's your father?"

"I don't know. No one has told me anything. The lady at the front desk just went back to get an update." Tears gathered in her eyes. She swiped them away. "I... I don't think it's good. Did you see him before they brought him in?"

"I did."

She noticed how he didn't elaborate. Her mind filled in the blanks, and it wasn't good. Nothing about this entire situation was good.

Kent's face was pale, and stress lines framed his eyes and mouth. "Why don't you sit down? It could be a long wait."

"I don't want to sit. I want to go back there and see him for myself."

Kent went to reach out and touch her shoulder but hesitated before lowering his arm. "I know it's hard. I wish there was something I could do. Sara would be here, but she's covering the inn for your father."

Melinda nodded in understanding. The truth was she didn't understand anything at the moment. It had been such a nice day, and even the evening wasn't so bad, because she knew by getting those books on the shelves as quickly as possible that it would bring such happiness to the group of hardcore readers that were constantly visiting the bookshop.

All it had taken was one phone call for her life to be turned totally upside down and out of control. She didn't like for things to be out of control. She liked lists and schedules. She liked to be able to know what was going to happen. This evening she didn't have a list, a schedule, or a clue what was going to happen next.

She glanced over as Kent took a seat. She didn't want to sit down, but at the moment, it appeared to be the only thing she could do.

Every time a door opened, all heads turned toward the treatment area to see if someone was coming to talk to them. For Melinda, time seemed to slow down. How could it take so long to check on a person's condition? What was keeping the kind woman from the front desk?

And then the helpful woman returned. Melinda rushed up to her. "How's my father?"

"They are still working on him. A doctor should be out shortly to speak to you."

Before she could say more, the door behind the woman opened. Melinda glanced that way and was relieved to see a friendly face. It was Liam Turner, Kent's younger brother. He was wearing his paramedic's uniform. She wondered if he was the one who'd helped her father.

When their gazes met, she saw exhaustion and worry in his eyes. She wanted to go to him and ask what he knew, but fear took root. What if he had bad news? Her feet refused to move. It was as though they were weighted down with concrete.

By then the woman had moved to the reception desk to check-in a new patient. Liam approached Melinda.

She swallowed hard. "Did you see my father back there?"

He nodded. "I was one of the paramedics that brought him in."

"How... How is he?" Fresh tears pricked the backs of her eyes, but she blinked them away. He glanced away, confirming her worst fears. Her entire body tensed, trying to keep her upright. "Is... Is he dead?"

Liam's gaze quickly met hers. "No." When her body sagged, he was there to catch her. He helped her over to a chair. Once they were seated, he said, "I won't lie to you. It's bad. His heart stopped twice. Once at the inn and once on the way here."

Melinda gasped as she pressed a trembling hand to her heart. Tears freely ran down her face. "Oh no."

"We got it started again."

A tear dripped onto her hand. "Will he make it?"

Liam paused. "They are doing everything they can. We'll have to wait and see."

As the tears streamed down her cheeks, Liam pulled her into his muscled arms and held her tightly. She let herself lean into his strong embrace. When his arms tightened around her, she felt safe and that all would be right in the world. It was a sensation she'd never felt before.

"Melinda?" The male voice drew her attention.

Melinda withdrew from Liam's embrace. She swiped at her cheeks before getting to her feet. It was Dr. William Mullins. He was the island's only full-time doctor, and it didn't help that he was of retirement age.

His gray hair was trimmed short, and a pair of black-rimmed reading glasses were perched atop his head. It was the worry lines bracketing his eyes and mouth that drew her attention.

She approached him. "My father... How is he?"

"He's had an acute coronary syndrome."

"A heart attack?"

The doctor nodded.

"How bad is it?"

"I can't give you a definitive answer, but we're going to rush him to another hospital with state-of-the-art equipment. They will be able to pinpoint the exact problem and hopefully be able to address it."

This was unbelievable. This was her father's life in the balance, and the only medical facility on the island didn't have the necessary equipment to treat her father. What if he didn't make it to the other hospital? What if moving him to the mainland was too much for him?

She halted her rambling thoughts. He was going to make it. And he would fight to hang in there. "I can't believe this place doesn't have the right equipment. When will you be able to move him?"

"We've been working to stabilize him." Dr. Mullins went on to tell her more about her father's condition. She struggled to take in all of the information when all she wanted to hear was that her father would be all right. "As soon as we have his vitals where we want them, we'll transfer him to the mainland."

"By helicopter?" When the doctor nodded, she asked, "Is it safe to move him?"

Dr. Mullins paused. "It's not ideal but it's necessary. We don't have the proper equipment here or the necessary staff to care for him. Trust me, you want us to move him as soon as possible. I really need to get back to your father. They'll be out with some paperwork that you'll need to fill out."

"I want to go with him," she uttered.

Dr. Mullins looked at her with sympathy in his eyes. "I'm afraid that won't be possible. There's no room on the helicopter."

"But there has to be. I'm his only family."

Liam reached out and took her cold, shaky hand into his own. "It's okay." His deep voice was steady. "I'll get you there."

Her gaze moved to the clock on the wall. "But the ferry isn't available now. And I can't wait for the next one."

"I understand. We'll take my boat."

The doctor told them which hospital they were transferring her father to before he moved back to the treatment area.

Once the doctor walked away, Melinda turned to Liam. "I don't want to intrude on your plans."

"You aren't. I don't have Tate. He's with his mother until next week. Let's get going." He turned to his brother. "Kent, let Sara know we'll be in touch with updates."

Kent nodded. "Let me know if either of you need anything."

"I need to grab a couple of things at my apartment. I don't know how long I'll be gone."

"We can do that on the way to the harbor," Liam said.

"Are you sure?" When he nodded, she threw her arms around him. "Thank you so much."

Melinda rushed out the door. Liam was by her side. She didn't speak as she quickly walked home. All the while her mind was focused on her father and figuring out how soon she could make it to the hospital to be by his side.

When she glanced at Liam, she noticed the worry that shone in his eyes. She didn't know if he was concerned about her or her father.

When they reached her apartment, she moved in a flurry of motion. She felt as though she was on automatic pilot, doing all of the necessary things in order for her to leave the island for a few days. All the while her mind was on her father, willing him to hang in there. He just had to live.

CHAPTER ONE

12 days before Christmas...

*J*INGLE. *J*INGLE. *J*INGLE.

On a cloudy Monday afternoon, festive Christmas lyrics filled the Seaside Bookshop. Melinda softly hummed along as she rang up a stack of children's books for Mrs. Harriet Moore. She was a frequent customer. And each time she visited, Melinda helped the older woman pick out the books for her great-grandchildren.

"Where's Ava today?" Mrs. Moore approached the checkout counter. "She's always so helpful when I'm here."

Ava Monahan was a junior at Boston University, where she studied business administration and played on the soccer team. She came back to the island often to spend time with her family and friends. Melinda was lucky that Ava was willing to work at the bookshop during the holidays and in the summertime when the tourist season was in full swing.

"She's taking the day off but she'll be back tomorrow."

"I'm sorry I missed her. Maybe I'll see her next time. But I'm happy to see you. How are things going?"

"Really well. The hospital fundraiser has been successful. I've arranged the Christmas bingo for Saturday to help with the building fund. Are you going?"

"I wouldn't miss it. I also heard that you were selected to decorate this year's tree for Twinkle Light Night. Congratulations."

"Thank you. It's such an honor."

"Any hints about how you're going to decorate it?"

Melinda smiled. "Sorry. You'll have to wait and see."

Each year the pine tree next to the town hall was tented the day before the tree lighting, and the sponsor was given twenty-four to forty-eight hours to decorate the tree. The locals made a big deal of trying to guess how the tree will be decorated.

When Johnson's Hardware did the tree a couple of years ago, the tree was trimmed in snowmen holding tiny wrenches, screwdrivers, and hammers. It was adorable. Last year, The Lighthouse Café did the decorating, and the tree was trimmed with lighthouses, candy canes, and miniature café coffee mugs. This year, Melinda was so excited to be selected to sponsor the tree.

She glanced down at the five books on the counter. "Did you find everything you were looking for?"

Mrs. Moore nodded her head as she held up a list. "You had all of the titles the kids want. It's going to be a special Christmas."

She rang up the books and told her the total. Mrs. Moore pulled out some cash and a bit of change from her navy-blue handbag. She handed it over. Melinda counted the money once and then twice.

"You're a dollar short," Melinda said.

"Oh, dear." She looked in her purse and frowned. "That's all I have on me. I'll have to put one of the books back." She looked perplexed as she thumbed through the little kid books."

Melinda thought it was so sweet the way Mrs. Moore doted on her family. "You know what? We'll consider it a friends and family discount."

Mrs. Moore shook her head. "You can't do that. If you do that all of the time, you'll go out of business."

She was right. "Okay. We'll consider this a one-time special."

"Aww...you're so generous. Your father is so lucky to have such a sweet daughter. How is Harvey doing?"

"He's good. I'll tell him you were asking about him." Melinda handed over the blue gift bag with white handles. "I'll see you at the tree lighting."

The woman's short-trimmed gray hair stayed in place she bobbed her head. "I wouldn't miss it."

Melinda smiled. "It's going to look epic."

"They said you were going to have a puppet show on Friday afternoon. Is that right?" Mrs.

Moore looked hopeful. When Melinda nodded, relief came over the woman's face. "Oh good. I will have all five of the littles while their parents do some holiday shopping. Sometimes they can be a handful, but now I will have something to entertain them." She smiled. "Thank you so much for all you do."

"You're welcome. I love to come up with special events. And it all pays off with the children's smiles." It was the truth.

Sure, the monthly activities at the bookstore kept people coming through the door and helped sales, but it wasn't the sole purpose for Melinda finding special events to do each month. Sometimes coming up with an idea was a challenge. But after a year of events, next year wouldn't be so hard, as she could repeat the events that worked and replace the ones that weren't well received.

As she watched Mrs. Moore make her way to the exit, she saw the door open. Cold air rushed inside the cozy shop. Outside, snowflakes fluttered through the air. Winter had settled over Bluestar Island.

Someone held it open for Mrs. Moore. Once the woman passed through the doorway, Melinda's father stepped into view.

There were shadows under his blue eyes. She noticed he was wearing his white hair longer than normal. And since he'd been released from the hospital, he'd grown a beard. If he wasn't careful, people might mistake him for Santa.

She couldn't believe it had been almost six months since her father had tiptoed on the line between life and death. It had been one of the scariest times of her life. Thankfully, they'd been given more time together.

Although, it had been touch and go for a while there. She couldn't help but think that if the island's medical center was replaced with a small community hospital with the ability to provide diagnostic tests it would be a huge benefit to Bluestar. What if the next time her father had a cardiac event, there wasn't time to get him to the mainland for the testing to know what treatment was needed?

She shoved the worrisome thought to the back of her mind because ever since that horrific night, she'd been doing everything in her power to make sure there wasn't a repeat event. Besides watching over her father, she'd taken it upon herself to begin a fundraiser to replace the medical center with an actual hospital with in-patient rooms. It was taking a lot longer than she'd like, but the process had been started.

Her father brushed the dusting of snow from his coat. He offered a brief hello to a couple of customers before moving on. In the past, he'd have spent at least five minutes catching up with those people. Her father used to be a talker, but not so much these days. It was tough adjusting to this new version of her father.

Melinda smiled. "Hi, Dad. What has you out and about on this blustery day?"

His lack of a smile dug at her heart. "I was out getting my afternoon walk."

"In this weather?" She worried about him. "You could slip and fall on the ice. And the cold air isn't good for you."

"Hush, daughter. Boy, is it warm in here." He unzipped his coat and took off his scarf.

Her father became distracted as a customer stepped up to the counter to check out a book. She wordlessly pressed her lips together.

Once she checked out Jimmy Shaw, she turned back to her father. "So, what has you stopping by today?"

"Is something wrong with a father wanting to check in on his daughter?"

"Of course not. You know I always love seeing you. And, if you're willing to hang around for a bit, after I close, we could go back to my place for dinner. When I heard the forecast for this week, I made some of that beef stew you love. I could warm it up. I might even have a loaf of fresh baked bread."

"You certainly know how to tempt me, but I'm afraid I already have plans."

"You do?" This was the best news she'd heard since her father was discharged from the hospital.

"Yes."

For the past several months, her father had lost his spirit. His usual bright shining smile was missing, and he'd become reserved. She'd been told that can happen after someone has a heart attack, not to mention the double-bypass he'd endured.

She'd done everything she could to cheer him up, but it hadn't worked. When he made it back to work at the Brass Anchor Inn on a part-time basis, she'd heard from her friend Sara Chen, who also worked at the inn, that her father was friendly and helpful with the guests, but he was different than he used to be.

Her gaze searched his. "Are you going to tell me what you're up to? Or are you going to make me guess?"

Her father arched a white brow. "I didn't know you were so interested. Maybe I'm the one that should be asking about your plans this evening. After all, I can't remember the last time you had a date."

"I told you I have too much to do. I don't have time for dating."

Her father frowned at her. "You're young and single. You should be out there dating and having a good time. The work will always be there."

She didn't want to discuss her lack of a social life. "We're talking about you. What's your plan for the evening?"

"I'm going to watch the hockey game."

It wasn't much, but at least he was showing an interest in something. He'd been a hockey fan her entire life. And he couldn't watch it at her place because she didn't have the sports channel. She just wasn't much of a sports person. She'd rather immerse herself in a good book.

"I'll drop off some stew after I lock things up here."

He shook his head. "It's okay. I've still got some of the pasta you dropped off the other day. I'll just warm it up in the microwave. I should be going."

"Love you, Dad."

"Love you too, kiddo." And then he strolled away.

Just then a young mother and her son moved to the checkout. Melinda couldn't believe how well the bookstore was doing with Christmas in the air. She made small talk as she rang up the children's books.

As they were walking to the exit, Melinda called out, "You forgot your scarf."

The mother paused and glanced at her daughter before turning back. "It's not ours."

Huh? It wasn't there earlier. She picked up the red knitted scarf. As her fingers touched the super soft material, she recognized it. This was the scarf she'd made for her father last Christmas. He must have forgotten it.

She rushed around the counter and headed for the door. She hurried outside. Hurrying outside, she was unprepared for the icy sidewalk. Her foot hit a patch, and her body fell forward.

Her arms slashed through the icy cold air as she struggled to regain her balance. She was losing the battle. And then her arms landed against something sturdy and unmoving.

In the blink of an eye, she realized it wasn't something but rather someone. When she tilted her chin upward, her gaze met a pair of striking blue eyes that reminded her of long lazy days on the beach while staring up at the clear blue sky. She knew that gaze. It was Liam. Embarrassment consumed her.

In her rush to straighten herself, she forgot about the ice. Her shoes slipped once more. Before she fell, Liam's hands reached out to her once more. His hands spanned her waist.

"Hey. Take it easy." His deep voice washed over her.

She stopped moving. "I'm sorry. I didn't see you. I was trying to catch up with my father."

Liam continued to hold onto her. "I didn't see him. Was it something important?"

She shook her head. "I suppose not." She held up the scarf. "He forgot this."

"I think he'll be okay without it."

"I... I'll drop it off this evening."

She realized he was still holding onto her. The heat from his bare hands radiated through her white sweater. It made her heart pitter-patter.

The reaction surprised her. It wasn't like they were anything other than friends—very good friends. However, they weren't going to be anything more than that. They'd both helped each other through tough times that year, and it had formed an unbreakable bond between them.

When she lifted her chin to look into his eyes, the words stuck in her throat. Sometimes, like this moment, she was struck by how handsome he was, with his blondish-brown hair, which he kept short, but it always seemed as though the strands were scattered like he made a habit of combing his fingers through it. His strong jawline covered with scruff. Her attention lingered on his lips. As soon as she realized she was staring, heat rushed from her chest to her cheeks. She glanced away.

She swallowed hard and hoped when she spoke that her voice wouldn't betray her straying thoughts. "You can let go."

He continued to keep a firm hold on her. "Are you sure?"

She nodded. "I'm really sorry about that. But thanks for the help."

"It was my pleasure."

There wouldn't be any more sudden movements. Of that much she was certain. With slow calculated steps, she made her way back into the bookstore. She needed to get some more salt for the sidewalk. She'd treated the walks earlier, but it'd snowed since then, and she suspected the temperature had dropped some more.

It seemed like Liam had a knack for always being around at the right time. She hoped he knew how much she appreciated his friendship. If anything good came out of her father's health scare, it was that it brought Liam into her life. She wouldn't do anything to risk their friendship.

CHAPTER TWO

L IFE CAN TURN ON a dime.

Or in his case with a snowfall—an avalanche to be exact.

Liam's life had drastically changed in the past few months. His ex-wife, Audrey, had handed over their son while she traveled to South America to go skiing. The sport had been her passion for her entire adult life. It wasn't exactly his thing. He'd only ever skied to please his ex.

They'd married young, perhaps too young to realize their fundamental differences. They were still naïve enough to believe love could conquer all. They'd been wrong but too stubborn to admit it to each other or themselves. They fought so hard to make their marriage work.

But when Audrey took a job as a ski instructor in Vermont, it was the beginning of the end for them. If he were honest with himself, they'd never been truly suited for each other. They didn't have any interests in common, except their adorable son. Tate had been a bridge between them, but by the time their son had turned one, the bridge wasn't strong enough to hold them together. Liam knew it. And Audrey knew it. Neither of them wanted to admit to their failure. In the end, she was the first one to vocalize it.

In the amount of time it took for a crushing amount of snow to race down a South American mountain, that was how quickly Liam and Tate's lives had changed forever. The fire station had Liam step away from being a volunteer paramedic to devote more time to his son as he coped with the loss of his mother and adjusted to his new life. Liam still couldn't believe Audrey was gone. And now he was a single father to a three-year-old. He had absolutely no idea how to be both father and mother to his precious son.

Liam pushed aside the troubling thoughts. He glanced over at Mel. "If you can point out where you have the salt, I can take care of the walks for you."

"I cleared them a little while ago."

"I can tell. It's just one of those snowy days where they'll have to be shoveled multiple times."

She nodded her head. Her long ponytail swished over her shoulder. Her cheeks still had a rosy hue. It looked cute on her. But there was this look in her warm brown eyes that caught and held his attention. He knew that faraway look. He'd seen it before when he'd kept her company in the hospital after her father's heart attack. She was worried about something, and he didn't think it had anything to do with the weather.

He raised his voice to gain her attention. "Mel?"

She blinked before focusing on him. "Um... You don't have to do the sidewalk."

"I know I don't have to do it, but I'd like to. Besides, I can't take the chance of a beautiful woman falling into my arms every time I walk past the bookshop." Now, why had he gone and said that? Although he did find her attractive—very attractive. And if he was in a position to date, he'd ask her out.

As the color in Mel's cheeks deepened, a smile pulled at the corners of her rosy lips. "I, uh... It's in the back."

And then he realized why he'd uttered those words—to make her smile. It warmed him like the sun, even though it was a cloudy day with snowflakes. No matter how challenging the day might be, when she smiled, it lifted his spirits. He followed Mel to the back room where she had a shovel and a bag of salt as well as a bucket.

He headed back outside. He cleared the steps and then salted them. The snow was wet and heavy. As he shoveled the walkway, he paused in front of the bookshop to catch his breath.

His gaze latched onto the picture window. He loved how Mel always went out of her way to create elaborate displays. This one was the theme from 'Twas The Night Before Christmas.

There was a Christmas tree with books standing beneath it. Each book had a red bow wrapped around it. Next to the tree was a cardboard fireplace designed to look as though it were made of red bricks. On the mantel were more books on display. There were stockings hanging from the mantel. And in the fireplace were black boots coming down the chimney. Santa was arriving with his bag of toys or maybe in this case a bag of books.

Liam's gaze was drawn back to the tree. He peered closely and found a little plush mouse with a sleeping cap and blanket, sound asleep under the tree. He let out a chuckle, shook his head, and went back to work.

He made short work of clearing the walk and salting it. He glanced up at the sky. The snow was coming down faster. It looked like for once the forecasters had gotten the forecast right—six-to-nine inches of snow by tomorrow morning.

After returning the shovel and bucket to the back of the store, he found Mel at the front of the bookshop. She was busy helping a little girl find a book about rabbits. He leaned against the checkout counter edged with garland and white twinkle lights. On the top of the counter was a small Christmas tree with all of the trimmings. Mel certainly enjoyed decorating.

He watched the interaction between Mel and the little girl as they searched for just the right book. Mel was so patient and kind. He could envision her being a mother someday. She would be such a good one.

The jingle of the little brass bell above the front door distracted him from his meandering thoughts. More customers entered the store. He knew the popularity of the Seaside Bookshop had a lot more to do with its owner than it did with the large collection of books. Mel had a gentle way with people, especially children.

A few minutes later, Mel made her way over to him. "I'm sorry to make you wait."

"It's no problem. Tate is over at my mother's place. She's baking some cookies."

"Sounds nice. I'm surprised you aren't over there taste-testing them."

"I will be after I leave here. I stopped by to talk to you about the furniture you wanted built for the remodel."

They'd worked on a drawing of the remodel of the front of the bookstore to distract her as her father slowly healed. She wanted something unique for the bookshop that made the most use of the space.

Her eyes lit up. "How's it going? Do you have the pieces completed?"

He rubbed the back of his neck. "That's the thing... I don't have the pieces done. And I don't know when I'll be able to complete them." He saw the disappointment in her eyes. "I'm really sorry. It's just with Tate and my work at the Blackwell estate, I've been running short on time."

"Oh. I see." The disappointment shone in her eyes.

It was just one more thing he felt as though he were failing at. He wasn't used to that feeling. As far back as he could remember, he'd always excelled at whatever he set his mind to.

But finding himself as the sole parent and trying to comfort his son had him totally out of his depths. It wasn't an excuse. It was the truth.

These days he pushed himself from the time he got out of bed in the morning until he collapsed in it after folding a load of laundry and watching the late show. He didn't have any more to give, and yet he wanted to help Mel. He really did.

"I just need to finish up my work at Blackwell's, and then I can focus on your project. I know I won't be able to get it done in time for Christmas. Not with the way Blackwell keeps changing what he wants from me." He leaned closer to her and lowered his voice. "Ever since he fell and broke his ankle, he's been even harder to get along with."

Mel was quiet for a moment as though digesting this information. She'd heard through the gossip mill about Blackwell's accident. "I'm so sorry. I don't really know the man, even though he's my landlord. When he stops by each month, all he says is, 'I need the rent.' He doesn't offer so much as a *hello* or *how are you*. Nothing that a normal, friendly person would say. Frankly, I'm surprised you were willing to take the job."

He didn't want to tell Mel that times were tough for his business. People weren't having custom furniture made like they used to, and with a child to support, he couldn't afford to be picky about his clients.

He was saving every spare cent for a down payment on a house. Tate needed more space than Liam's one-bedroom could provide. And a backyard would give his active son room to move around and burn off some of his endless energy.

"What can I say? The pay was right. Of course, it's the insurance company picking up the tab after the storm damage at the mansion."

"I remember hearing about it. So, you're helping with the restoration work?"

He nodded. "A lot of the woodwork was destroyed. Right now, I'm working on the staircase and banister."

"I'm sure it'll look beautiful when you're done."

He rubbed the back of his neck. "I hope so. That guy doesn't have one nice word to say. All he does is nitpick everything. It doesn't matter how hard I try, it's never up to his expectations."

Mel reached across the counter and covered his hand with her own. She gave him a squeeze before she pulled away. "You do amazing work. Don't let Blackwell get to you."

She was right. It was just with all that had happened lately, he felt the weight of the world on his shoulders. "Thanks for the kind words."

"They aren't just words. They're the truth."

They'd been casual friends before her father's heart attack, but the traumatic experience bonded them in a way that would last a lifetime—at least he hoped so. Mel had become his best friend. He never wanted that to change.

CHAPTER THREE

11 days before Christmas...

BLUESTAR LOOKED MORE LIKE Christmasville than a beach town.

The following day, Melinda smiled as she strolled along the sidewalk. The sky was blue, and the sun was shining bright. The snow storm had moved on, but there was still a chill in the air. Each breath she exhaled created a cloudy puff.

The shops along Seashell Drive were all decked out for the holidays. One had a Christmas village display in the window. Another had a small Christmas tree trimmed with miniature ornaments. And yet a different shop had plush cartoon characters in a scene of them decorating a Christmas tree. She loved how each shop took a different approach to decorating. She had joined in the fun with her rendition of *'Twas Night Before Christmas*. She might have cheated and taken the idea from this year's children's play.

She was grateful it hadn't snowed overnight because her arms were still sore from the numerous times she'd had to shovel the heavy snow the day before. She couldn't wait to get inside and warm up. Spring wouldn't arrive soon enough.

"Brr... It's another cold one."

Melinda glanced over to find Aster Bell approaching her. Her friend was bundled up in a red coat with a white scarf and gloves. Aster was the island's event planner. Since she took the job a couple of years ago, she'd done an amazing job of breathing life back into the island. And their tourism numbers had soared.

Aster's rounded belly peeped out from the jacket. She was due to give birth any day now. Mel was surprised to see her out and about, especially on such a cold morning.

"Good morning." Melinda sent her a smile. "What has you out and about in this chilly weather?"

"I actually came to see you."

Melinda's brows rose. She hadn't been expecting to speak with Aster until well after the New Year, when Aster returned from maternity leave. "Then by all means let's take this conversation inside where it's much warmer."

"Agreed."

Melinda unlocked the front door and flipped the light switches on the wall. Row by row the ceiling lights flickered on. The shop always seemed too quiet in the morning. She enjoyed the hustle and bustle of customers coming and going throughout the day.

Melinda slipped off her boots and pulled a pair of flats from her red and green holiday tote. She picked up her boots and then turned to Aster. "Come on. I'll make us some coffee." She rushed to the back and put her things in the office before returning to the front. "I should have asked if you drink coffee?"

"Normally, yes. But I'm not drinking caffeine until this little one arrives."

She nodded in understanding. "Is there anything else I can get you? Maybe some hot tea."

"No, thanks." Aster's gaze lowered. "I don't have much time, but I wanted to stop by and let you know the town council met last night." She fidgeted with her purse strap.

"I didn't realize they were meeting so soon. Should I have been there?"

Aster shook her head. "It wasn't necessary, or I would have called you. This was their final meeting of the year."

Melinda could see by the way Aster's brows were drawn that there had been a problem at the meeting. "What happened?"

"You know how we have new council members?" When Melinda nodded, Aster said, "Well... The board is more interested in growing Bluestar's economy and bringing in more tourism than building a hospital."

There was a distinct sinking feeling in the pit of her stomach. "What does this mean for the hospital project?"

"They voted against it."

Melinda planted her hands on her hips. "So that's it? They're just doing away with the plan for a new hospital? You know it wasn't just me who worked on this plan. There were former council members. We had an architect and a contractor. Did they even look at our proposal?"

Aster paused as though gathering her thoughts and perhaps giving Melinda a chance to calm down. "They know. They don't care. There isn't going to be a new hospital. I'm so sorry."

Mel knew Aster truly felt bad about the situation because when she'd first approached her about raising money for the hospital, Aster had been very supportive of the idea and had gone with her to speak to the mayor, the former council, and had helped set up the various fundraisers.

"But they can't just take that money and use it for whatever they want. The money was raised with the intention that it would medically benefit the community."

"I pointed this out to them and was informed the money could be used to expand the current medical center by adding another bed or two to the examination area."

"Another bed or two? That's not enough for Bluestar. If they hadn't noticed, the population is growing, not shrinking. We need better health care, especially preventive care."

Aster nodded in understanding. "I totally get where you're coming from. And I emphasized this at the meeting, but they were resolute."

Melinda gestured with her arms as she spoke. "So that's it? The hospital is just scrapped."

"Not quite."

Hope bloomed in Mel's chest, but she refused to get excited until she heard what was involved. "So, the idea isn't completely dead?"

Aster shook her head. "It's a long shot, but it's the best I could do. You have until the New Year to secure the necessary funding for the hospital project."

Mel's mouth dropped. "But that's impossible."

"That's why I said it was a long shot. I'm really sorry about this." Aster's face scrunched up in pain as she put a hand to the small of her back.

Thoughts of the fundraiser were sidelined as Melinda grew concerned about her pregnant friend. "Come." She gestured to a chair. "Sit down."

Aster shook her head. "Thanks. But it's not worth it. Trying to stand back up these days takes a herculean effort. If I just give it a moment, the pain will subside."

Mel gasped. "Are you in labor?"

Aster once more shook her head. "I thought the same thing. We rushed to the medical center and were informed it's Braxton Hicks contractions. It's just practice for the real thing."

"It'll all be worth it when you're holding that little baby in your arms."

Aster smiled. "Yes, it'll all be worth it. I can't wait. And now I have to be going. I have some other stops to make."

"You're still working this close to your due date?"

She nodded. "I promised Sam this would be my last day. I tried to talk him into going to Twinkle Light Night tomorrow, but he told me I needed to put my feet up and rest." Aster's gaze met hers. "I'm so sorry. I really wanted to be there."

"There's nothing to be sorry about. I agree with your husband. Take care of you and that baby. You've done an amazing job with organizing the holiday calendar. Everyone will enjoy themselves."

"Thank you." She pressed a hand to her rounded abdomen. "I just wanted to go and see how you decorated the tree."

"I'll send you a picture."

"That would be wonderful. Thank you." A pleased smile came over Aster's face. "Let me know if there are any problems."

"You should be on maternity leave. Surely there has to be someone to fill while you have the baby."

"I wish, but I don't have an assistant or anything."

Melinda nodded in understanding. "I'll let you know, but I don't think you have anything to worry about. Everything this holiday season is going to run smoothly."

"Thanks. And I will rest. It'll make Sam happy. And hopefully, the baby will show up tomorrow."

Melinda smiled at the way Aster's face lit up every time she spoke of the baby. "Have you let the baby know it's to make an appearance tomorrow?"

"Yep." She pressed her hands to her rounded abdomen. "They know. It's time to come out and see the world."

"Do you know if it's a boy or girl?"

She nodded. "But we aren't telling anyone until they're born."

"I guess we'll find out soon."

They hugged, and then Aster made a quick exit. Melinda was left with the thought that all of the work she'd done in the last six months to help create a hospital with a surgical unit and diagnostic testing equipment was about to be a total waste, unless she could come up with some sort of Christmas miracle. She didn't have a clue how to make that happen. She reached for her phone to call the people who'd helped get them this far.

CHAPTER FOUR

IT WAS SLOW, PAINSTAKING work.

Liam knelt next to the staircase. He slid a piece of wood in position. He ran his hand over the smooth surface. This project was keeping him from taking on other jobs, like handmade furniture for his family's furniture store as well as the pieces for Mel's bookshop. But being a single parent, he couldn't afford to turn down any jobs.

He'd worried about money since Tate was born. There was nothing cheap about raising a kid. And now that Tate lived with him full-time, he needed to get them a bigger place. It was no easy task. Housing on the island was hard to come by. When something became available, he had to be financially ready to pounce.

Not so long ago he had his ex there to help with everything concerning their son. Because somehow they'd made it through the divorce and come out the other side as friends.

He missed Audrey. Not as his wife, but as a co-parent and friend. He missed their chats about Tate. He missed her "chill-lax" attitude. He didn't know many women that were low-key like her.

Maybe if she hadn't been so low-key, she wouldn't have taken a risk on the slopes and ended up buried alive in an avalanche. He'd never know.

In the meantime, he had to try to figure out how to be both father and mother to Tate. Each day he felt as though he wasn't living up to that responsibility. Each day he promised himself he would do better. Each day ended with him feeling as though he hadn't accomplished enough.

He shouldn't have agreed to work for cranky Horace Blackwell. The man was hands down the grouchiest person on Bluestar Island. It was the reason Liam had gotten the job—no one else had wanted it.

He knew why nobody else wanted the job. Blackwell didn't have a nice word to say to anyone, but working for him was even worse. The man couldn't start his day without threatening to fire Liam. No one had ever treated him so shabbily. He was a well-respected craftsman, but you could never convince Blackwell of that.

So, today he'd been replacing the staircase that had been damaged in the storm when part of the roof collapsed. The roof should have been replaced years ago, but miserly Blackwell didn't want to spend the money. Now the insurance company was paying for a new roof and redoing most of the second floor. All the while, Blackwell nitpicked about everything. He was angry that the repairs were taking too long. The man was totally and utterly exasperating.

But Liam didn't have to think about Blackwell for the rest of the day. He picked up his tools and made his way out the door, all the while avoiding Blackwell. As he drove off in his cart, he breathed a sigh of relief.

Next on his agenda was delivering a piece of furniture he'd been working on. It would give him some extra money, and he had a treat in mind for Tate.

The delivery didn't take long. And then he was off to his mother's house to pick up his son. He found them in the living room, playing with interlocking blocks. Tate had a very determined look on his face as he pressed a red brick and a yellow one together.

Liam stopped at the doorway and watched for a moment. He couldn't help but smile with the way his mother was willing to get down on the floor to play with his son. It appeared she was building a house.

His gaze moved back to his son. He wasn't sure what Tate was making. As though his son sensed his father's attention, he turned his head and smiled. He held out the various colored bricks. "Truck."

Liam didn't quite see a truck in what his son had created, but that didn't stop him from smiling. "Good job. Are you ready to go home?"

"No." Tate gave his head a quick shake before picking up more bricks.

When Liam's mother went to stand, he moved to her side in order to give her a hand up. Not that his mother needed his help. She was still quite spry. He supposed it had to do with living on Bluestar Island. Aside from the sunshine and fresh air, there was the fact that walking was greatly encouraged because cars and trucks were banned from the small island, unless you received a special permit from city hall. And generally they were hard to come by.

"I need to talk to you." There was a note of seriousness in her voice.

He straightened. "What is it?"

"I heard from Uncle Jim this morning. Your aunt Susan fell."

"How bad is it?"

"Luckily, nothing is broken, but she's pretty banged up. They won't be able to make it for Christmas." When he nodded in understanding, his mother said, "Your father and I were talking. None of our siblings are getting any younger. And this latest scare with your aunt has us thinking that we need to make more of an effort to spend time together."

He nodded. "Of course, you should."

Her gaze moved to Tate. "It will mean you'll have to find someone to watch Tate."

His mother had been great about watching him. So great in fact that he'd kept putting off finding other daycare. He certainly couldn't ask his mother to stay because of his procrastination.

"Don't worry. I have him enrolled in Storybook Daycare."

Relief replaced the worry in her eyes. "Charlotte Davis owns it. She is so nice and quite competent." Her gaze moved to Tate. "But do you think he's ready for another big change?"

It's the reason he'd been hesitant to take Tate to daycare. It seemed like everything kept changing for his son. "I don't know, but we're about to find out."

"Maybe we shouldn't go. I'll just explain to your aunt and uncle that we can't make it. I'm sure they'll understand."

"No. Don't do that. I've got this." It was a lie. He felt as though he was juggling everything and trying not to drop any of his responsibilities. "I might even take some time off. After all, it's the holidays."

"But how will Mr. Blackwell feel about your time off?"

"Does it really matter? That man is never happy." Liam would still honor his agreement with the man, but he was so tired of Blackwell constantly changing his mind about the shade of stain or every other detail. "Don't worry, Mom. Everything will be fine. This will be good for Tate. He'll make some new friends. And that's what we want, isn't it?"

"Of course." She sent him a hesitant look. "Are you sure?"

"I'm positive. Now let me clean up these toys so we can get out of here."

Five minutes later, the toys were placed in a wooden toybox, which Liam had made and his ex had painted. They'd given it to his parents when he and Audrey had announced they were expecting Tate. He remembered that day so clearly. It was like it'd just happened yesterday. It was so hard to believe how drastically things had changed in the span of four years.

Liam gave himself a mental shake as he scooped up his son in his arms. "Thanks, Mom."

"Anytime. You know how much I love spending time with Tate." She lifted up on her tiptoes and pressed a quick kiss to Tate's cheek.

"And you'll be home for Christmas?"

"We wouldn't miss it. Love you."

"Love you too." He headed out the door.

Once he had Tate secured in his car seat in the covered golf cart, they set off. There were a few snowflakes in the sky, but not enough to cause problems with the roads. But he wasn't ready to head home just yet.

Liam turned up the fan on the heater. "Warm enough?"

"Yeah." Tate chattered about the little truck he pulled out of his pocket.

They were on their way to the Seaside Bookshop. He'd promised Tate a new book. His son loved books. At night, Tate couldn't pick just one for a bedtime story, He'd choose four or five. Liam's mother said Tate was just like him at that age.

Liam wanted to encourage his son's love of reading. He made a point of reading Tate at least one book each evening. They'd read his small collection of books a number of times already. He planned to expand Tate's library this Christmas.

As they neared the bookshop, both sides of the street were filled with carts covered with a light dusting of snow. Finally, at the end of the block, he found a spot and zipped into it before some other Christmas shoppers could snag it.

He slipped Tate's mittens on and pulled up the zipper on his little blue coat. He wanted to carry Tate, but his stubborn, independent son insisted on walking. Hand in hand they made their way to the bookshop.

"We're going to the bookshop. What sort of book would you like to get?" Liam asked. "One about a train?"

"Fire engines!"

Liam smiled. His son loved fire trucks. They were his favorite toy. It was why there were at least six of them at home. Each was a different size or different color. Tate played with them every day. He hadn't met a fire truck he didn't like.

"What about a Christmas book?" When Tate didn't respond, Liam said, "You know a story about Santa? Or how about some reindeer?"

Tate glanced up at him with wide eyes. "I like Rudy."

Liam smiled at his son's shortened name for Rudolph. He had a problem pronouncing the reindeer's full name. "Me too. We'll have to see if they have a book about him."

The prior evening they'd watched Santa's reindeer on television. Tate had been mesmerized by the flying reindeer. And then there was the one with the glowing nose. Tate had proceeded to pinch his own nose. And when he got bored of that, he'd climbed onto Liam's lap to pinch his nose. Repeatedly. And hard. The kid was definitely strong for his age.

Liam gripped Tate's hand tightly as they made their way up the steps to the bookshop. Tate was adamant that he could climb the steps. It was a challenge for his little legs, but he did it without any mishaps.

When Liam opened the door to the bookshop, the aroma of chocolate greeted them. He inhaled deeper. Mm... The hot chocolate smelled amazing and perfect for this cold, snowy weather.

Liam stomped off his boots on the extra-large welcome mat in front of the door. When Tate saw what he was doing, he mimicked his father's actions. Liam couldn't help but smile, but he also realized the enormity of the moment. Tate was watching his every action and listening to everything he said. The pressure to be not only a good parent but also a good human being weighed on him. Because whatever Tate saw him do, his son was going to imitate. And he wanted his son to grow into a compassionate man.

"Hey, guys."

Liam turned his head to find Mel standing several feet away. When their gazes met, a smile lifted her lips and lit up her eyes. The warmth of her smile immediately warmed him up to the point where he yanked down the zipper on his coat.

"Hi. We came to buy a book." His gaze moved to his son, who was pulling on his zipper too. "Didn't we, Tate?"

The little boy silently nodded as he looked at all the books.

"First, we should take off your jacket."

When Liam reached for his son's jacket, Tate said, "I do."

Tate tugged on the zipper. When the zipper got stuck, Mel rushed forward and knelt down in front of him before Liam could react. She talked to Tate about Christmas as she worked to free the zipper. All the while his usually shy-with-strangers son talked to her.

When Mel had the zipper undone, she straightened. Tate shrugged off his coat. Liam caught it just before it fell to the wet mat. He breathed a sigh of relief because he didn't need any more laundry to do. He already had two heaps of dirty clothes and towels.

Mel's gaze moved from his to Tate's. "What sort of book are you looking for?"

"Rudy!" Tate smiled at her.

When Mel turned a confused look in Liam's direction, he said, "He means the reindeer."

"Yeah." Tate clapped his hands.

Liam turned to his son. "Your mommy loved reindeer too."

"I like Rudy," Tate said.

"It's good that you talk to him about his mother," Mel said. "It'll give him a chance to know her through your eyes."

"I try."

"I have some reindeer stories over here." She gestured to the display near the shop's big window as she looked at Tate. "Would you like me to show you?"

Tate eagerly nodded his head. And then to Liam's great surprise, when Mel held out her hand to Tate, he slipped his little hand in hers. Liam had no idea that they'd bonded. He couldn't blame his son for liking Mel. She was the best.

Tate glanced back at him. "Daddy."

"I'm coming." Liam followed them to the Christmas display.

As Mel talked to his son and showed him a book, Liam took the time to glance around. This front section was the area she wanted to turn into a reading nook area—a place where customers could take their book purchases and read. And with the giant picture window, what better advertising could you have than people reading and enjoying books.

He smiled when his gaze landed on her Christmas display with Santa's boots sticking out of the chimney and the sleeping mouse under the Christmas tree. She certainly had some imagination. Of course, he already knew that since he'd been drawn into her plans for the bookshop's refresh project.

The pieces of furniture she wanted for the area didn't exactly have a traditional look. He was excited to work on the project because it would test his skills.

Tate let out a giggle. It filled Liam's heart with hope that they'd get through this rough time, and he would somehow figure out how to be the good parent his son deserved.

"Daddy, look!" Tate pointed to a bright, colorful picture of a reindeer.

He knelt down next to his son and pointed to the picture. "Who is that?"

"Rudy."

Liam couldn't help but smile. "Do you like Rudy?"

Tate's head bobbed up and down.

"Why don't you take it over to that table and look at it?" He didn't have to say it twice as Tate made a beeline for the red and white children's table that sat next to the wall. Liam turned to Mel. "Thanks for that. He loves the book."

"It wasn't hard. It's the most popular book with the littles this year."

"If you have a couple more like it, I'll take those too."

Mel's brows briefly rose. "Christmas presents?"

He shook his head. "I'm starting him in daycare tomorrow. It'll be another big change for him, and I feel bad. I thought some new storybooks would cheer him up."

She studied Liam for a moment. "I'm not sure that it's your son that needs the cheering up."

"What does that mean?"

Concern shone in her eyes. "You just look as though you have the weight of the world on your shoulders."

He sighed. "It's nothing."

"Well, I'm here if you need a shoulder to lean on or an ear to listen. After all, I owe you big time for how you helped me after my father's heart attack."

He shook his head. "I've told you that you don't owe me anything."

"Then let me be a good friend."

His gaze met hers. "You already are."

A smile bloomed on her beautiful face. It set his heart a thump-thumping. In that moment, his worries about Mr. Blackwell, Tate's first day at daycare, and the staggering pile of laundry faded into the background.

He couldn't help but smile back. There was just something special about Mel. It was probably why her bookshop was so popular.

Jingle-jingle.

It was the little brass bell above the front door. Both of them turned to see Sara Chen enter the shop. Sara's gaze panned the store until she spotted Mel. She waved. And Mel held up a finger to let her friend know that she'd be just a moment.

When she turned back to him, he said, "We should get going. I have some laundry that needs my attention." And then he turned to Tate, who was showing another little boy the reindeer book. "Tate, let's go."

"Oh. Your books," Mel said. "Do you still want them?"

He'd forgotten all about the other Christmas books. He'd let himself get distracted by Mel. It wasn't hard to do. Her smiles were infectious. And she was easy to talk to.

When he noticed her looking expectantly at him, he cleared his throat. "Yes. Please."

"Do you have anything particular in mind?"

Liam shook his head. "Whatever you think would suit Tate."

When she moved to the bookshelf, he went to gather his son, who still hadn't moved from the little table. "Are you ready to go home?" When Tate ignored him, Liam said, "We can go home and look at more books. Would you like that?"

Tate nodded his head. "Can we look at *all* the books?"

"I don't know if we'll have that much time, but we can look at some of your books."

"The truck books?"

Liam smiled. "Yes. We can look at the truck books."

With a little more negotiating, he was able to get Tate's coat on him, pay for the books, say goodbye to Mel, and then they headed out the door. He regretted having to leave so soon. He enjoyed spending time with Mel, but he had responsibilities awaiting him at home, and Sara seemed anxious to speak with Mel. He wondered what that was about, but it was none of his business. After all, he and Mel were just friends.

CHAPTER FIVE

10 days before Christmas

I T WAS ALL UP to her now.

Melinda had talked to everyone that had worked on the hospital project. They'd all agreed on one thing: it would be impossible to raise that large sum of money in such a short span of time.

She'd reminded them about the pending funds from the state, but their thoughts were hung up on raising the remaining balance. Melinda had to agree that without winning the lottery, she had no idea how she'd come up with the money by New Year's. The thought continued to plague her. This project was too important to just give up on, but what other choice did she have?

But for the moment, she was happily distracted. While Ava managed the bookshop, Melinda had spent all day decorating Bluestar's Christmas tree in the little park next to the town hall. It was a huge honor to do it. A white tent had been erected over the ten-foot evergreen. Sara Chen, Kent Turner, and her father had assisted her.

She'd wanted to ask Liam to help, but she didn't want to disrupt his day at the Blackwell estate. She didn't know how he could work for that grinchy man. She figured Liam must really need the money, and there was no way she was going to make him choose between earning a living and helping out a friend.

Luckily her father had thought to bring along some space heaters. Inside the tent, the heaters definitely took the edge off of the cold. It was far from warm, but with their coats on, it was comfortable.

Her legs ached from climbing up and down the ladder countless times. And even though she'd been on her feet all day, her step count had only reached something like eight thousand steps. How was that possible? She felt as though she'd been walking all day.

At last the tree was trimmed, and it didn't look half bad, if she did say so herself. She was so excited for the town to see it that evening at Twinkle Light Night. She'd worked for months to come up with just the right look. And it'd turned out even better than she'd imagined.

And now that it was late in the afternoon, it was time to head back to the bookshop. Sara rode with her. Melinda was relieved to find that the holiday business had been steady. It appeared that half of Bluestar Island's residents would be receiving books that Christmas. They'd sold a lot of kid's books and for the adults, cozy mysteries had been a big hit. In fact, she made a mental note to place an order for more who-done-its.

After she thanked Ava for handling the shop while she'd been decorating the tree, she gave Ava the rest of the day off. When Melinda perched on a tall stool behind the checkout counter, she sighed. She was so happy to at last be off her feet. Liam had made her the stool as a birthday gift. He told her she didn't always have to be on the go. She'd used it plenty of times in the months since he gave it to her.

"Melinda, did you hear me?" Sara's voice interrupted her thoughts.

She blinked and glanced at her friend. "What did you say?"

Sara frowned at her. "We didn't get to talk much earlier. What's up with you today? You've been distracted all day."

There was no way she was admitting that she had been thinking about Liam and Tate. She knew Sara would jump to all of the wrong conclusions, especially now that Sara and Kent were an official couple. Sara now seemed to think that everyone should have a love match. But Melinda didn't have time for romance—not that she'd ever had much luck when it came to cupid's arrow.

Melinda swallowed. "I was just thinking about something Aster told me."

Sara's eyes lit up. "How's she doing? Isn't she supposed to give birth anytime now?"

"Would you believe she was still working?"

Sara nodded. "I can believe it. She's always on the go. Doing this or that. She has more energy than five people."

"Aster said she's taking time off now until the baby comes, but she wanted to update me on the town council meeting." A frown pulled at the corner of Melinda's lips.

"Oh no. It doesn't look like it was good news."

"Far from it. They want to shelve the idea of building a hospital on the island."

"How can they do that? You've already raised a lot of money for it. Plus, the people on the island want and need this."

"I agree. But with a bunch of seats on the council being turned over, apparently the new council is more interested in bringing in more tourists and less interested in the health of their local residents." Anger pumped through her veins. She never wanted anyone else to go through what she'd dealt with her father. Of course, she knew there was no way to avoid all heart attacks, but she had to believe with more available healthcare on the island it would help a lot of people.

"I'm really sorry. What are you going to do now with the money?"

She noticed Alice Lewis approach the checkout counter with a book of knitting patterns. Melinda held up her finger to Sara and then moved to the register. After some chit-chat about the weather and the tree lighting scheduled for later that evening, she handed Alice her purchase.

Once they were alone, Sara asked, "What are you going to do? There has to be a way to change their minds."

"Aster already did her best to convince them to stick with the plan, but they're intent on scrapping it." She sighed. "I just can't believe they're doing this. Don't they understand how important it is to have a better equipped medical facility and to have specialized doctors here on the island?"

As she thought of her father having another heart attack and not having the time to be life flighted to the mainland, her breathing came faster in shorter gasps. Her heart felt as though it were racing. And her palms grew clammy. What would she do without him?

She loved her father a lot. After the death of her mother, it'd just been the two of them. They spent every holiday together. And since his heart attack, she made a point of spending more time with him. She tried to go every Sunday to his place to cook healthy meals for the week so he'd have meals in the fridge ready to be rewarmed.

"Hey." Sara sent her a worried look. "Are you okay?"

Melinda blinked a few times. She wouldn't give into the panic, because this fight wasn't over yet. "I'm fine."

Sara looked at her hesitantly. "Are you sure?"

She nodded. "This isn't over yet."

"What does that mean?"

"Well, Aster argued with the council until they gave us a small window to make this hospital a reality."

Sara arched a brow. "How small is this window?"

"Very small. I have until the New Year to secure the necessary funds."

"As in a year from now?"

Melinda shook her head. "No. As in the end of the month."

Sara's mouth gaped. "How are you going to do that? I mean you've been working on this for what? Five months? And you still have a long ways to go."

The thought of failing made her chest tighten. There had to be a way to do this. She just didn't know what the answer might be.

"I've already applied to the state as well as for some federal grants. I'm waiting to hear back on those." She'd been waiting for quite a while now. She could only hope that people would want to clear their desks before the holidays, and she would get an answer by Christmas.

"Will that be enough money?"

Melinda shook her head. "No. I still need a lot more money. And I have no idea how to get it. The people of Bluestar have already been so generous."

"And don't forget we have the Christmas bingo coming up on Saturday night. We've sold so many tickets that they had to talk to the fire department about how to squeeze more people in the building."

Melinda couldn't help but smile. She was so grateful for all of the wonderful people who lived on this island. When there was a problem, they chipped in and helped out. But there were a few that put their own interests ahead of everyone else. And it appeared they'd been elected onto the city council.

"I wish the money raised by the bingo would be enough, but it's not even a drop in the bucket. I need to come up with a lot of money and really fast."

"Do you have a rich uncle or grandparent?"

Melinda shook her head. "I wish."

"So let's think, who on this island is rich?"

Melinda strained her brain trying to come up with someone with deep enough pockets to be able to help. And then a name came to her. She immediately rejected it.

"By the frown on your face," Sara said, "I bet you thought of the same person that I did."

"Trust me. Horace Blackwell won't help."

Sara shrugged. "How will you know until you try?"

Melinda sighed, and then she lowered her voice, even though there were no customers in the bookshop at the moment. "Because you know as well as I do that Blackwell doesn't help anyone but himself."

Her thoughts turned to her landlord. She'd been informed last month that he was increasing her rent for the bookshop—a lot. He was trying to get rid of her. He hadn't bothered to hide the fact. She let him know she had no interest in going anywhere.

She honestly couldn't afford the increase in rent, but she'd do what she could to increase business. She wasn't going to be forced out by a bully who thought he could get people to do what he wanted by force. No way.

"He really is a curmudgeon."

"He's worse." But after the stories she'd heard over the years about how he'd made his fortune on the stock market all the while living in his family's mansion, he could afford to supply the remaining funds they needed. Still, it wasn't going to happen. The man was so miserly that it was pathetic. "And after breaking his ankle, you'd think he'd be anxious for better care on the island."

"Maybe you should ask him." Sara's gaze probed her.

"No—"

"You can't write him off until you ask him. Maybe he's had a change of heart."

Melinda resisted the urge to roll her eyes. "First, he'd have to have a heart."

"I know you're tempted." Sara's voice interrupted her thoughts. Her gaze moved to the clock behind the counter. "It's closing time. Why don't we drive by his place?"

Melinda's eyes widened. "You're volunteering to go talk to him with me?"

Immediately Sara shook her head. "Not a chance. That guy scares me."

Melinda frowned at her. "But it's okay for me to talk to him."

Sara nodded.

This was a bad idea. But now that Sara had planted the seed of an idea, it continued to grow in Melinda's mind. She had to at least ask him.

"Fine." She sighed. This was going to be a total waste of time, but he hadn't been around to pick up her rent check yet. If she didn't get it to him before the end of the week, it would be late. "I have to drop off my rent."

"There you go. You have the perfect opportunity to speak to him." Sara smiled, as though she'd somehow solved the problem.

"You have to know there's no way he is going to donate. He's a penny-pincher from way back."

"I would like to believe there's some good in his heart."

Melinda couldn't help but smile as she shook her head in disbelief. "You're the most optimistic person I've ever met."

Sara's smile broadened. "Thanks. Now let's get going. I have to meet up with Kent in a little bit."

Sara helped Melinda close up the bookshop. All the while Melinda kept telling herself this was a bad idea—a terrible idea. But she wouldn't be able to rest until she'd exhausted all options—even the most improbable.

After flipping to the *closed* sign on the door and locking up, they drove toward the Blackwell mansion. It was already dark out. The days were so short at this time of the year.

"Are you going to the tree lighting tonight?" Melinda asked.

"I wouldn't miss it. I'm so proud of you. Kent and I will both be there. Are you going with anyone special?" Sara waggled her brows as she smiled.

"You know I'm not dating anyone." She hadn't dated anyone since her father's heart attack.

"What about Liam?" Sara looked pointedly at her. "If you married him, we could end up being sisters-in-law."

Heat swirled in her chest, rushed up her neck, and set her cheeks ablaze. "Sara, stop! I can't believe you said that."

"I'm just pointing out the obvious."

"Obvious to whom?"

"Anyone with eyes that sees you two together."

"What? No." She shoved away the thought. They were friends. Nothing more. "Besides, I can tell when a guy is interested in me, and he's not."

"If you say so."

Melinda mentally shook off her friend's words. There was no way Liam was interested in her. They were friends. That was all. Why did people think it was impossible for a man and woman to just be friends?

The Blackwell mansion was situated on the edge of town. As they approached it, Melinda was surprised by how neglected the estate had become. There were overgrown evergreens and shrubs that had overtaken the black wrought-iron fence and blocked the view of the large gray Victorian house with black trim.

"It didn't used to be this way." Melinda gestured to the mess. "I remember when I was a kid, the grounds were immaculate. I don't know what happened for it to end up like this."

They parked and got out. They followed the fence, searching for an entrance. They made it to the driveway without finding a gate.

Melinda turned to Sara. "Did I miss the gate?"

Sara shook her head. "I didn't see it either, but did you see all of those no trespassing signs? That was a lot."

Melinda nodded. She resisted the urge to say she wasn't surprised. Blackwell was not a friendly person. "It's so strange there's no gate. How does he get deliveries?"

Sara gestured to the side of the driveaway. "There's an intercom. Try it."

"I don't know." Melinda was having second thoughts about all of this.

"Hey, we drove all of this way. You can't back out now."

"It wasn't that far." But then she recalled the rent payment in her pocket. She expelled a resigned sigh.

She moved to the intercom and hesitated for a moment. Then she realized she was being silly. It wasn't like the man was going to shout at her for dropping off her rent payment. In fact, he might be grateful. It was one less stop he had to make.

She pressed her finger on the button. Nothing happened. She waited. When no voice came on the intercom, she pressed the button again. And again.

She couldn't help but wonder if it was broken. If that were the case, how was she going to reach Blackwell? The thought of climbing over that tall fence with those pointy ends was not inviting at all.

"Go away!" A raspy voice crackled from the speaker.

Melinda jumped. She hadn't expected to have someone yell at her. She didn't need to see his face to know she was speaking to Horace Blackwell.

She swallowed hard. "Mr. Blackwell, this is Melinda Coleman. I came to speak to you."

There was a slight pause. "Are you moving out?"

"No." She had absolutely no intention of giving up her lease for the bookstore. She loved the shop, and once she made the modifications to it, the bookshop would be perfect. The only drawback was her landlord.

"Then go away."

"Please, Mr. Blackwell, if we could just talk."

"Leave now! Or I'll call the sheriff."

Wow! The man was even worse than when he came around to collect her rent. But she wasn't about to just give up. If she could just get past the gate and talk to him in person, she could plead her case for building the hospital.

She raised her hand to press on the intercom button again, but before she reached it, Sara reached out and stopped her. When Melinda turned to her friend, Sara shook her head.

"I don't think it's a good idea." Sara lowered her hand.

"This is ridiculous. It's not like he's actually going to call the sheriff."

Sara arched a brow. "Are you sure about that?"

Melinda opened her mouth to respond but then wordlessly closed it. In all honesty she didn't know Blackwell. And she really didn't want to face the sheriff. Something like that would be certain to make it to the gossip mill, and that was all sorts of the wrong publicity.

With a resigned sigh, Melinda said, "You're right. I'll try again another time." She turned to head back to her cart. When Sara didn't follow, Melinda asked, "Aren't you coming?"

"I think I'll head over to Kent's place. It's not far from here. I'd like to grab some dinner before the tree lighting."

"Okay. I'll see you there."

As Melinda drove away, she pondered how to approach Blackwell. She supposed she could wait until tomorrow when he would be around to collect the rent. Suddenly, tomorrow seemed so far away.

She checked the time. It was just after five. Instead of going home to eat alone, she decided to surprise her father and have dinner with him. Since his heart attack, she'd tried to make more time for him. It wasn't always easy with her own business to run, but she hoped in the new year to be able to hire an assistant.

Her steps quickened as her evening plans took shape. She'd head to the Lighthouse Café and pick up dinner for the both of them before heading to her father's place. At least this way she'd know he was eating healthy. A smile pulled at her lips. Her father always hated when she fussed over him, but without her mother around, the job fell to her.

CHAPTER SIX

PHONE CALL MADE.

Liam ended up talking to the daycare's voicemail. He let them know he'd be dropping Tate off in the morning. He'd been paying them to hold the spot for more than a month. It was finally time to let his little boy take the next step and make some new friends.

Next, he got to work on the household chores. He started the laundry before he loaded the dishwasher. Once he got going, he kept going.

Toys picked up. Check. At least for the moment.

Vacuum run. Check.

Bedding changed. Check.

Liam didn't have time to hang up the clean clothes. He'd do it later. He also needed to make a run to the grocery store. The fridge was bare, and the cabinets weren't much better.

As though he read his father's thoughts, Tate walked over to him and pulled at his shirt. "I hungry."

Hungry? Liam turned to the wall clock. It was after five. The afternoon had gotten away from him.

"Hey, Tate, do you want to go get a burger?"

Tate shrugged his little shoulders.

"What about some fries and ketchup?"

Tate nodded his head. He loved french fries.

Buzz.

Liam pulled his phone from his pocket. When he saw the name of his son's new daycare, he figured they were calling him back to let him know some last-minute details like what to pack in his backpack or to include snacks.

He pressed the phone to his ear. "Hello."

"Liam, this is Jane Givens at Storybook Daycare. I really hate to do this, but we won't be able to take Tate tomorrow."

"I don't understand. I thought we had this all worked out. I did the paperwork, and I've paid so that his spot would be there when he was ready. Well, he's ready."

"It has nothing to do with any of that."

"Then I don't understand."

"His teacher has come down with a severe case of pneumonia. She's going to be out of work until after the holidays. I'm really very sorry."

"It's okay." No, it wasn't. He didn't have a backup babysitter. "I hope she's feeling better soon."

"Thank you. We are hoping the same. I feel really bad about this. Will we see Tate in the New Year?"

"Yes." He didn't hesitate. He'd been assured that Storybook was the best daycare on the island, and it wasn't their fault his teacher had gotten sick.

Jane gave him names of a few people who might be able to take Tate until the New Year.

They talked a little more before saying goodbye. As Liam slid the phone into his back pocket, his mind raced as he tried to find a solution for this problem. There was absolutely no way he was going to tell his mother about this new development. He knew she'd cancel her trip, and that was the last thing he wanted.

He might still be figuring out how to be a full-time father, but that didn't mean he was going to become a burden on his parents. He'd get through this somehow. If he could just find a babysitter.

He tried the names Jane had given him, but he was too late. All of the spots had been filled by other children from the daycare. He had to come up with an alternative.

And then he thought of the bulletin board at the Lighthouse Café. It was a community board where people posted all sorts of things from items for sale to apartments for rent to help needed, and sometimes there were postings from people looking for work. He could only hope that some of the college kids were home and looking for some work over the holidays.

While Tate played with his small fire truck as he sat in his booster seat, Liam drove his covered cart to the restaurant. A few snowflakes fluttered through the night sky. It wasn't enough to mess up the roads. It put a white dusting over the bushes, trees, and sidewalks. It smoothed out the rough edges and made Bluestar look like a winter wonderland.

All the parking in front of the café was taken. Liam wasn't surprised. The Lighthouse Café was one of the most popular spots on the island. Liam's family had spent many meals at the restaurant from celebrations to sharing an after-football game meal. He'd even had his first date here.

He found a parking spot down the street. When he went to pick up Tate to carry him to the café, Tate strenuously insisted that he could walk. So hand-in-hand or rather hand-in-mitten they made their way along the sidewalk. Liam said a casual greeting to the passersby.

Once inside, Liam moved to the huge bulletin board that was used by the locals. His gaze scanned over all of the apartments currently available. In the winter, housing wasn't much of a problem, but come the springtime, all of the places on the island filled up quickly. He moved past the used carts for sale as well as the washer and dryer and various other household appliances that someone could pick up at a reasonable price.

Tate yanked on his arm.

"Hang on, Tate. I'm almost done." At last his gaze landed on the job openings.

He scanned the little pieces of paper one at a time. None of them said anything about babysitters or nannies. He sighed.

Tate pulled harder on his arm. "Okay, buddy, let's get you some fries."

"Yeah!" Tate pulled his father into the café.

He glanced around, noticing that the café wasn't overly decorated for Christmas, unlike many of the other places in Bluestar. The café's walls were painted a beachy blue with ocean murals. But there was a miniature Christmas tree on the long counter at the back of the restaurant.

The spacious dining room was filled with small wooden tables and chairs made of whitewash wood. On every tabletop was a lighthouse ornament. It had a little wreath affixed to it. And the top of the lighthouse glowed. It wasn't over the top, but it was something. Liam could deal with it.

Just then Helen Bell came up the walkway toward them. When her gaze landed on Tate, Helen stopped in front of them. "Hi, Tate."

Tate backed up, running into Liam, who put a reassuring hand on his shoulder. "Tate is being a little shy today."

Helen nodded. "For now. But someday, I bet he'll be a heartbreaker." She turned her attention back to Tate. "And what did you ask Santa for Christmas?"

"Santa?" Tate's little voice touched Liam's heart.

There was so much he had to teach his son from Santa Claus to respect and so many other things. In that moment, he felt Audrey's absence from their son's life. She would have been so much better at teaching their son about life's lessons. But Liam had made a promise to himself that he would do everything he could to be a good parent—the best parent he could be.

And if today was any gauge, he wasn't doing so well. He either found a babysitter tonight, or he wouldn't be able to work tomorrow. If he didn't work, he didn't get paid, and there were bills to pay.

"We'll discuss it later. Okay, buddy?"

Tate nodded his head.

"He's just the cutest. Merry Christmas." The woman moved past them toward the exit.

The café was busy. He gazed around the room, and when he spotted an open table, he scooped Tate up into his arms and made a beeline for it before it was taken.

He shrugged out of his black coat and placed it on the back of the chair. At that moment, a server came over with a wooden high chair—one of the chairs he'd crafted for the café. It always gave him a funny feeling on the inside when he spotted people using the items he'd made. He was so thankful that people appreciated his work, and it allowed him to do what he loved—work with his hands. He just loved the smell of fresh cut wood.

Once they were seated at the table, Tate began coloring the back of his placement with one of the crayons supplied by Lucy, their server. Liam perused the menu. He didn't know why he bothered. He had the menu memorized, and he always got the same thing—a bacon double cheeseburger with everything and fries. Tate was like him and ordered a kid's burger and fries.

Time was running out. He had to figure out an arrangement for Tate's care for the remainder of the week and next week. He recalled how his siblings had offered to help out with Tate after Audrey had died. He'd never taken them up on the offer because he'd been so busy proving to himself that he could manage everything.

He glanced over at Tate to find him coloring on the table. Liam struggled to keep from sighing. Tate had a habit of coloring everything but the paper, including their walls and his high chair. Luckily, the tabletop had a clear coating that was resistant to crayons.

He reached out, placing his hand over his son's tiny hand. "Hey, we don't color on the table. Color on the paper, or I'll take your crayons away."

Tate didn't say anything, but he did pull the placemat closer and continued to color on it. Liam knew he'd have to keep a close eye on his son as long as he had the crayons. Who knew what Tate was going to color next?

Liam leaned back in his chair and looked around. He spotted Mel walking in. He waved at her. Immediately, her face lit up with a smile. It was exactly what he needed after a long day.

Her smile was radiant and lit up her whole face. Even her big brown eyes twinkled. In turn, it made his heart beat faster, and there was this spot in his chest that grew fuzzy and warm. There was something so very special about her.

Still, if he were to start something with her now, he'd just mess it up because his time was not his own. And most of all, he couldn't afford to lose their friendship when things ended. He counted on their friendship. He needed her in his life.

The idea of asking her to babysit sprang to mind. It was definitely tempting. After all, he trusted Mel implicitly. And Tate liked her too. And yet he dismissed the idea as quickly as it had come to him.

Mel was just getting her life back to normal after caring for her father. And she was so busy with the holiday season that he hesitated to impose on her.

Liam waved her over. When she reached the table, she said, "Hey, Tate, whatcha doing?"

"I color." He lifted the placemat to show her the scribbles of purple and yellow crayon.

Her face was animated when she said, "Wow! That's really pretty. I love the purple."

Tate put the placemat back on the table and picked up the purple crayon. He continued to scribble.

Mel turned to Liam. "We keep running into each other today."

"Join us."

She shook her head. "I'd love to, but I can't. I have to pick up some food before I head over to my father's. We're having dinner before going to the tree lighting. You're going, aren't you?"

He leaned back in his chair as he raked his fingers through his hair. "Honestly, I totally forgot about it. I'm sorry. I've been so busy."

The light in her eyes dimmed. "Oh. I understand."

"Melinda." Lucy approached her. "Your order will be a couple more minutes."

She nodded in understanding. "Sounds good."

After Lucy moved on to another table, Liam said, "You might as well have a seat while you wait."

"I think I will." Mel pulled out a chair and had a seat. She glanced at the three-year-old. "There's a rumor that Santa will be there tonight."

Mel really seemed to be getting into the holiday spirit, whereas for him, it was just another day—at least that was how it'd felt since his marriage was on the rocks and after the divorce. Unless he had Tate, he often avoided as much of the town's calendar of events as he could.

And right now, he had other things on his mind—like finding a babysitter for Tate. Otherwise, he was going to have to explain to Blackwell why he couldn't work the next day. He didn't think the conversation would go well.

CHAPTER SEVEN

THERE WAS A FLICKER of something troubling in his eyes.

In a blink, it disappeared.

Melinda was left to wonder what was on Liam's mind. By the frown lines marring his handsome face, it couldn't be good. Her heart went out to him.

After her father's heart attack, they'd developed a close friendship. He'd made a point of checking on her at least once a day. Sometimes he phoned. Sometimes he would stop by. And sometimes he'd bring her food.

So, while she had taken care of her father, Liam had been taking care of her. When she resisted his outpouring of kindness, he told her she couldn't take care of her father if she didn't take care of herself.

Their friendship continued to blossom. She would tell him about her day, and he would tell her about his. It was so easy to talk to him. And soon they were each other's confidants.

And then it had come as a shock when Audrey had tragically died in a skiing accident. Tate had come to live with him full-time. Now it was

Melinda's turn to check in on Liam each day and remind him to take care of himself so he was able to care for his son. But lately Liam had grown quieter and more reserved with her. It was as though he were building a wall between them, and she didn't understand why.

She wanted to tear down the wall between them. She missed her friend. He understood her in a way that Sara and Ava didn't. And he never pushed her—not unless he was worried about her.

But she was worried about him. He was mourning the death of his ex-wife. Even though he rarely mentioned her, he must still be in love with her. Maybe he'd been hoping that Audrey would come back to him, and now that dream had been stolen from him. As his friend, it was her duty to help him through this difficult time.

She rested her elbows on the table. "Please, say you'll come tonight."

He shook his head. "I'd like to, but I have things I should do."

And then she had a thought. "Does your hesitation have something to do with you not being able to help me decorate the tree?"

His shoulder had a slight lift and fall. His gaze didn't meet hers as he said, "It's just this big job with Blackwell has kept me busy, and now there's Tate. I didn't mean to let you down."

"But you didn't. I totally get that you're busy. I was never upset with you." She hoped this would clear the air between them.

Lucy stopped by the table. "Melinda, your food is ready. It's on the counter."

"Thanks. I'll be right there."

After Lucy moved on, Liam glanced at Tate, who'd covered most of the paper by now with various colors of crayons. "Tate?" He waited until he had the boy's attention. "Would you like to go see the Christmas tree lighting tonight?"

Tate hesitated and then nodded his head.

Liam turned back to her. "We'll be there. I can't wait to see how you decorated the tree."

"You won't be disappointed."

There was still something weighing on him—something he wasn't saying, but now wasn't the time to try to break through his protective layers. Maybe tonight at the tree lighting, they'd get a chance to speak again.

He shouldn't have agreed.

He had other matters that needed his attention.

Liam had broken down and called his siblings. His sister, Josie, was happy to help. She couldn't watch Tate at all this week, but she could take him the following week. His younger brother Jack could watch Tate this Friday but not tomorrow. And his other brother Owen didn't pick up.

If he didn't find someone to watch Tate tomorrow, he wouldn't be able to work. And if he didn't show up for work tomorrow, he had no doubt Blackwell would fire him. He couldn't afford to lose this job.

He scooped Tate up in his arms as he rushed toward the park. They were late. His brother was unusually chatty this evening, and it was difficult to get him off the phone. It was almost like he knew Liam had to be somewhere, and he had set out to delay him. Though that was impossible because he hadn't mentioned the tree lighting ceremony, and Jack wouldn't have guessed he'd be here, because this wasn't his sort of event. He didn't get caught up in the holiday festivities that overtook the island at this time of the year.

When they stepped into the crowded park, he found the tree was already lit up. They'd missed the big moment. Guilt settled over him. All he could do now was find Mel to apologize and hope she'd forgive him.

In the background "O Christmas Tree" played. This was the beginning of the big run-up to Christmas day. It wasn't far off.

When he finally got a clear view of the tree, he was impressed. Mel certainly had a creative mind. The tree was trimmed in white lights with large shiny red ball ornaments. But the other ornaments were what drew his attention. There were miniature book ornaments. There were bikes, dragons, and various other shapes. Each shape had a quote from a book. There was a skinny white banner near the top that read: *Let your imagination take flight.*

The entire tree was decorated and at the top was a silver star. Although the tree was only ten feet tall, it still would have taken a lot of work to get it all done. And he should have figured out how to make time to help her. Instead, he'd worked and tried to please a man who was incapable of appreciating anything. He banished the thought of Blackwell. He wasn't going to let that man ruin both his day and his evening.

"You're here!" The familiar voice came from behind him.

He turned to find Mel smiling at him. He blinked just to make sure he hadn't imagined the happy look on her face, but it was still there. Maybe she didn't know he'd missed the tree lighting.

He wanted to gloss over his lateness, but his conscience wouldn't let him. "I'm so sorry we're late."

Her gaze searched his. as though she could read his thoughts. He hoped she could see how bad he felt. He knew she would never be late if the roles had been reversed. That realization only made him feel worse.

"It's okay. I know if you could have been here, you would have." Sincerity rang out in her voice. She turned to the tree. "What do you think?"

"You did a fantastic job." He looked at the tree, always seeing something new. "How many of those ornaments did you make?"

She shrugged. "A few."

He knew it was a lot more than a few. Mel liked to be in control of whatever she did. She was certainly talented.

"Maybe you could take up ornament making on the side."

She shook her head. "Between the bookshop and my father, I wouldn't have the time." Her expression turned serious. "I need to talk to you."

Before she could say more, they were interrupted by people wanting to congratulate her on such a great job with the tree. Normally, he would have meandered off and let her have this moment in the spotlight, but considering he had missed the big moment, he couldn't just disappear. He didn't want her to think he didn't care. Nothing could be further from the truth.

And so he stood there smiling when appropriate and nodding at just the right times. In between, Tate would point to something on the tree, and Liam would talk to him about it. Tate wiggled in Liam's arms, trying to get down, but Liam wasn't comfortable with letting him down in the crowd.

Just then his brother stepped up next to them. "Hey, Jack. What are you doing here?"

"After you mentioned it on the phone, I decided to swing by and see what's going on." His gaze turned to Tate. "Hey, buddy."

"Unc Jack!" Tate still struggled to pronounce his L's.

His brother took Tate into his arms. "You're getting big."

"Tell me about it," Liam said. "He keeps growing out of his clothes. He's going to need 5Ts for Christmas."

"Did you see Santa yet?" Jack asked.

Tate shook his head.

"Would you like to?"

Tate wordlessly shrugged.

"When I was your age I would tell him what toy I wanted for Christmas, and then it would appear under the tree on Christmas morning. Would you like to give it a try?"

Tate nodded.

The three of them were about to walk in the direction of Santa when Mel's voice drew Liam's attention. "I'm sorry about that."

She said hello to Jack, and he complimented the tree. It all felt so natural, as though the four of them hung out all of the time. Or maybe that was just what he wanted to happen.

"Liam, could I have a private word?"

Jack gestured with his head. "We'll just be over there, visiting with Santa."

Once they were out of earshot, Mel said, "I heard you are in need of a babysitter."

He struggled not to roll his eyes. He should have known his inquiries would make it to the Bluestar gossip mill. "His teacher at the daycare is sick, so they're shorthanded and can't take him until after the holidays."

Mel nodded in understanding. "So, my question is why didn't you ask me? From what I've heard, you've been asking everyone else."

Disappointment shone in her eyes. "Don't you think I'd make a good babysitter?"

"What? No." And then realizing how that might sound, he stammered, "Wait. That isn't what I meant. I mean, I think you'd make a good babysitter."

Her eyes lit up with amusement. "Then, why didn't you ask me?"

"Because..." His mind raced for an answer that wouldn't get him into more trouble. "You have to work too. With the bookshop, you won't have time to keep after an active three-year-old."

She crossed her arms. "So, you don't think I can do more than one thing at once."

He sighed. He wasn't walking into another word trap again. "Mel, stop. That isn't what I think. I just didn't want to impose."

She was quiet for a moment. "Is that really the only reason?"

"Of course."

"Good. Then drop him off at my place tomorrow morning on your way to work. We'll hang out there until it's time to open the bookshop."

It all sounded good to him. He just hoped this wouldn't put a strain on their friendship. That was the last thing he wanted, but he did need to work. His thoughts drifted to the house he hoped to purchase in the near future.

Chapter Eight

9 days before Christmas

W HAT HAD SHE BEEN thinking?

She'd overcommitted herself.

The following day, Melinda had been on her feet all day as she watched over Tate and oversaw the bookshop. Thankfully, Ava was there to help her out. Who knew a three-year-old had an unending supply of energy. If only she could be half as energetic as Tate, she could accomplish so much.

Melinda had been hurt when she'd heard Liam had seemingly asked everyone else on the island but her to watch over Tate. She felt as though their friendship was growing more distant by the day. And that was why when she saw him at the tree lighting, she'd pushed the point.

Her gaze moved to Tate as he sat at a small table by the checkout counter. He was the sweetest little boy. She could see he was a bit withdrawn from the other kids that came in with their parents, but she hoped with some time he'd find his footing and make some new friends.

Luckily, Liam had thought to pack some of Tate's favorite toys. She kept those in the office area. When she worked on the computer, Tate could play on the floor next to her desk with his monster trucks. And when they were out front, she gathered some books for him to look at. She learned that he was quite good with his numbers, shapes, and animals.

The day hadn't been exactly perfect. There had been some spilled apple juice, a ripped page in a book, and running through the bookshop until he ran into a customer. But none of it had been earth-shattering. In fact, Melinda had been pleased with how well things had gone.

"He's adorable." Ava stood next to the checkout counter and smiled as she watched Tate point at the pictures in the book. "Someday, I hope to have a little boy just as cute as him."

Melinda arched a brow. "Shouldn't you finish college before you start daydreaming about little ones."

Ava blushed. "Uh... Yes. I was just daydreaming about the future."

She wanted to ask if Ava had a certain guy in mind to be the father of her imaginary baby, but she refrained. She didn't want to embarrass the girl any further.

Ava was a beautiful young woman with long brown hair that she usually pulled back in a ponytail while a curtain of bangs framed her sweetheart face. Her warm brown eyes were emphasized with eyeliner and eyeshadow. Not enough to be obnoxious, but just the right amount to show off her expressive eyes. It wouldn't be long until some young man came along and stole her heart. Melinda was surprised it hadn't happened yet.

There were no more customers in the shop, and it was ten minutes until closing. "Why don't we close a little early? After all, tonight is the ice-skating party."

"Are you sure?"

Melinda moved to the front door and turned the *open* sign to *closed*. "I'm positive. Are you going to the party?"

Ava nodded as her cheeks once more took on a rosy hue. "Jason asked me to go with him."

"I take it you like Jason."

Again Ava eagerly nodded her head. "I liked him all through high school, but he never seemed to notice me."

"And now he has. I'm happy for you."

"Thanks. I could really use the extra time to get ready for our date tonight."

"Then quit standing around here and get going. I'll close up."

"Thank you." Ava rushed to the back of the shop to grab her coat and boots. As she rushed to the front door, she said, "You're the best."

"Just don't go rushing home. It's icy out there."

"Now you sound like my mom."

Ouch! She wasn't anyone's mother. Her gaze moved to Tate as he pushed his trucks over the floor. The thought wasn't without its merits, but she didn't have time to be a mother right now with a growing business to manage and a stubborn father to worry about.

Melinda waved to Ava. "Maybe I'll see you later."

Instead of making Liam walk to the bookshop to pick up Tate, she messaged him and let him know they'd meet him at the Blackwell mansion. After all, she wasn't giving up on speaking to him. She still had the rent check to hand over.

Tate was a sweetie as he helped Melinda pick up his toys and put them in the backpack Liam had sent with him. She knelt down next to him. "Thank you for your help."

"Welcome."

Her heart melted every time he used his manners. "Shall we go see your daddy now?"

Tate eagerly nodded his head.

Normally, she would have walked to the Blackwell place, but she didn't want to keep Tate out in the cold any longer than necessary, so she'd driven her cart to the mansion. The cart was covered and had a little heater that fit conveniently in the cup holder. It wasn't perfect by any stretch, but it was a lot better than being out in the blustery cold air.

She made chit-chat with Tate, who only responded now and then. She wondered if he had always been so quiet or if it had something to do with his mother's sudden death. She couldn't even imagine what it must be like for a three-year-old to try to comprehend that he was never going to see his mother again. The poor little guy.

"Look." Melinda pointed. "There's your daddy."

Tate sat up straight in his seat and gazed out the window. "Daddy!"

She pulled to a stop on the side of the quiet road. Snow gently fell in large lazy flakes. Liam strode over and opened Tate's door. "Hey, buddy. How was your day?"

"I played with trucks."

"You did?"

Tate smiled and nodded his head.

Melinda loved watching how Tate lit up around his father. There was no need for words when it came to father and son. The love between them was on display for anyone to see. Tate held his arms out to his father as Liam released the booster seat.

Melinda got out and joined them on the sidewalk. "Someone is happy to see you. Aren't you, Tate?"

Tate rested his head on his dad's shoulder and let out a yawn.

"I think he's tired," she said. "He played hard today."

"Did you have fun today, Tate?"

"Uh-huh."

"So same time, same place tomorrow?"

Liam arched a brow. "Actually Jack offered to take him, so you're off the hook."

"Oh." She was surprised by the level of disappointment that came over her. She chose not to examine the origin of her disappointment. Instead she smiled at Tate. "That's too bad. I enjoyed our time together, but I know you'll have fun with your uncle Jack."

"Between you and me," Liam said, "I was surprised that Jack sounded genuinely interested in hanging out with Tate."

Melinda followed them to Liam's cart. "Hey, Liam, are you going to the skate party at the Apple Blossom Farm this evening?"

"I wasn't planning on it."

"Oh. Okay." She struggled to keep her disappointment from showing on her face.

"Why? Did you need something?"

She shook her head. "It's nothing like that. I was just hoping there'd be someone there I know."

He smiled. "Mel, you know everyone in town."

"I know, but I was hoping there'd be someone there I could hang out with and just be me."

He cleared his throat. "Maybe I could see if my neighbor is available to watch Tate for a little bit. She has a son about his age, and sometimes they play together."

She didn't want him to go out of some sort of obligation. If he went, she wanted it be because he wanted to be there. "You don't have to do that on my account. I'll be fine."

"No. I'm doing this because I haven't had an evening off in months. And last night I got caught up on the house work. Finally. Do you want me to pick you up?"

The thought appealed to her, but she didn't want to put him any further out of his way. She shook her head. "I'll meet you there."

She held Tate while Liam put in his booster seat. She gave Tate a quick hug before handing him over to his father to be secured in the seat.

While Liam did that, she moved back to her cart and retrieved the backpack with Tate's toys. As she returned, Liam stood waiting for her. The snow dusted his brown hair. There was some scruff along his strong jawline. But it was his blue eyes that captured her attention and held it.

He was staring directly at her. When their gazes met, her heart skipped a beat. There was something different about the way he was looking at her. What was he thinking?

As she came to a stop in front of him, her heart beat too quickly. She swallowed hard as she held the backpack out to him. "Here you go."

At last he broke the gaze as he took the backpack from her. "Thanks. I really appreciate you doing this."

"No problem. I really enjoyed our time together. He's a very sweet boy."

He hesitated. "I guess I should get going."

She nodded. "I should too." She pulled a white envelope from her purse and held it up. "I have to drop off my rent."

His brows lifted. "Are you sure you want to do that? Blackwell's not in a good mood."

She sighed. "Is he ever in a good mood?"

"True." Liam smiled. "Do you want me to go with you?"

It was sweet of him to offer. "Thanks. But I've got this."

"Are you sure?" Worry shone in his eyes.

"Of course. It's not like he's going to attack me or anything. All he has are his words, and I can deal with those."

He hesitated. "Okay. Well, good luck."

She waved as they drove off. Tate waved back at her. She smiled. He was just the sweetest. And his father wasn't so bad either, especially now that he wasn't freezing her out. She was happy he'd agreed to go skating. A leisurely evening was what they both needed.

But first she had to deal with Horace Blackwell. She turned and gazed through the overgrown shrubs and weeds lining the wrought iron fence. Between the vegetation, she could see a dark gray house with black trim. The paint was peeling, and the windows were clouded with dirt and cobwebs.

It would certainly make a good haunted house. There was absolutely no holiday cheer about the place. It filled her with an unsettled feeling, but she wouldn't let that stop her. She had to do this.

CHAPTER NINE

S HE SHIVERED.

Melinda stared up at the Blackwell mansion. She couldn't state for certain if the bodily reaction was from the icy breeze rushing past her or the knowledge that she was about to face the crankiest man on Bluestar Island. It didn't matter what the real answer was, because nothing was going to keep her from asking him to help the town.

She crossed the driveway and pressed the speaker button. She stuffed her gloved hands into the pockets of her coat as she waited. Another ocean breeze rushed past her, making her teeth chatter. She pressed the intercom again. She kept her finger there longer than was necessary because the cold was creeping past the warmth of her jacket, making her teeth chatter.

She quickly pressed the button again. Holding it. Holding it. Holding it. And then she let up.

"What do you want?!"

His harsh voice caused her to jump. "I... I have my rent money."

"Put it in the mailbox." His voice almost had a growl to it.

"No. I want to hand it to you."

"Mailbox."

She blew out a frustrated sigh. What was it with this man that he felt as though he could just brush her off? Doubts settled in about asking him for the money for the hospital. But she'd come this far; she wasn't going to be turned away at the gate. She had to at least ask him.

What would he do if she were to march up to the door? It'd be harder for him to turn her away if he had to do it face-to-face. The more she thought about it, the more the idea appealed to her.

She moved toward the gate and glanced around until she spotted the entrance off to the side of the driveway. She walked over to it. It was most likely locked up tight, but it didn't stop her from gripping the black wrought iron and giving it a push. It had a tiny bit of give so she tried again.

This time she used both hands and pushed with all her might. The gate screeched as metal rubbed against metal. To her surprise, the gate swung open.

She stepped through the opening and stopped. She half-expected an alarm to go off or a big mean guard dog to rush toward her. None of that happened.

The little hairs on the back of her neck lifted. She could feel someone staring at her. She scanned the big old house. She noticed the slightest movement of a curtain in a first-floor window.

Blackwell was watching her. Well, she wouldn't disappoint him. She marched over to the walkway, which hadn't been shoveled. It didn't surprise her. Blackwell was known to be a penny pincher. She stepped in what she assumed were Liam's footsteps. She should have worn boots, but she hadn't anticipated making her way through a foot plus of snow.

She trudged up to the door, tracking snow across the porch. She rapped her knuckles on the door. To her utter surprise, the door was immediately yanked open.

Horace Blackwell stood there with a scowl on his unshaven face. His sparse gray hair in desperate need of a haircut was in disarray. "You're trespassing."

She pretended not to hear him. "Hello, Mr. Blackwell. How are you?"

"I'd be better if you hadn't snuck in here. It was that Liam. He let you in. He's fired."

Oh no! She hadn't expected the man to jump to such an outrageous conclusion. "Liam had nothing to do with me being here."

"I don't believe you. He can forget getting paid. He's done here."

"Stop it! You know that isn't true."

His gaze narrowed behind his black-framed glasses. "I saw you break through my gate. I can have you arrested."

She pursed her lips as she chose her words carefully. "If you saw me come through the gate, then you also saw that I was alone, and Liam had already left with his son."

Her unwavering gaze challenged him. He could be such a bully, but she wasn't afraid of bullies. And she certainly wasn't afraid of him. Something told her he was more bark than bite.

"What are you doing here?" His words were sharp and pointed.

"I brought your rent payment."

He arched a brow. "Is it the new amount?"

The grinch of a man had raised her rent this month. He'd been vocal about the fact that he wanted her to move out. He had other plans for the building the bookshop was in, but she wasn't giving up her store. Not a chance. It wouldn't be easy to meet the higher rent, but she would make it work.

"Yes, it is."

The frown lines deepened on his face. He reached out for the envelope, but she yanked it out of his reach. "Not so fast. We need to talk."

"You need to give me that money and get off my property before I call the sheriff."

If anyone else had said those words to her, she would have been shocked, but coming from Blackwell, it was just part and parcel of his mean-guy spirit. "Go ahead. I'll just wait here."

The man's mouth opened but then wordlessly closed. His bushy gray brows were drawn together, forming a menacing look, but Melinda wasn't falling for all of his bluster. She wasn't afraid of him.

"What do you want?"

She glanced down at the walking boot on his lower leg. "I was sorry to hear you got hurt. How are you doing?"

"I'd be better if you would leave, and I could put my foot up."

And now she had found the opening she needed to discuss the proposed hospital. "You must have to take trips to the mainland to have your foot looked at, don't you?"

"What of it?" His gaze once again narrowed.

"I was just thinking that in this winter weather and with your cast that it must be hard on you."

"Life is hard. What of it?"

"You know, if we had a small hospital here on the island, you wouldn't have to make that long trip. You could just pop into our very own hospital and have everything taken care of there."

He was quiet for a moment. Did that mean he was considering the idea? Dare she let her hopes rise ever so slightly? After all, this was Horace Blackwell, the cheapest man on the island—probably the cheapest man in Massachusetts. It wouldn't surprise her if he was the cheapest man in the country. But her grandmother had told her money wasn't everything—you certainly couldn't take it with you when you died.

His bushy brows rose above the black frames of his glasses. "I know what this is. You want to shake me down for money for that hospital fundraiser.

Well, you've wasted your time. It's not going to happen."

Her heart sank. "Please reconsider. It's really for a good cause—a cause that can help you."

His gaze darkened. "I don't need your help or anyone else's help."

Was he serious? He was on crutches. And with the way he wobbled, he wasn't so steady on his feet.

"Is there anything I can say to change your mind?"

He shook his head. "Now, get out."

Really? She'd never met anyone so rude in her life. Thank goodness. One Horace Blackwell was more than enough.

How was she ever supposed to get through to him? Something told her that this whole visit was a total waste of time. Yet, she had to try and now that she had, it was time to make her exit.

He might take the low road but she refused to. "Thank you for hearing me out." She turned to walk away when she recalled the rent payment. She stopped and turned back just as he was closing the door. "Wait. I forgot something."

The door paused, but she noticed it didn't open wide again. "What is it?"

She held the white envelope out to him. "Here's my rent. I didn't want it to be late." She glanced down at his cast. "It doesn't look like you'll be able to pick it up on your own."

He snatched the envelope out of her hand so fast it hurt her fingertips. She smothered a frustrated groan. That was the last time she hand-delivered her rent. If he didn't pick it up next month, she'd mail it to him.

Without another word, she turned and continued to the steps. It wasn't until she was on the bottom step that she heard him call out her name. She wasn't sure she wanted to stop and deal with more of his grumpiness. He was probably going to complain about the rent and insist he was going to raise it yet again.

She took another step down onto the snow-covered sidewalk.

"I have a proposition for you."

She hesitated. Was this some sort of trick? What proposition would he have for her? And did it have anything to do with the hospital fundraiser?

She knew if she didn't find out what he was talking about, it would continue to bother her. And so she turned around, but she didn't climb the steps again. "What proposition?"

"It's cold out there. Come inside."

He was inviting her inside his house? This must be big. But why hadn't he mentioned it when she was at the doorway? After a lingering moment, she retraced her footsteps.

Once just inside the door, he said, "I'll make you a deal."

She was quiet for a moment. She refused to let him think she was overly eager to deal with him after the way he'd spoken to her. And there was the fact that she had absolutely no idea what he had in mind.

She lifted her chin and met his gaze. "What do you have in mind?"

"As you can see, I can't go out in this weather. I need someone to pick up all of my rent payments that are due now."

He wanted her to be his assistant? Seriously? She could think of a million other things she'd rather do. It wasn't like this man had ever gone out of his way for her or anyone else that she knew in Bluestar. In the next breath, she realized she didn't want to be like him—greedy and self-centered.

As though he sensed she was hesitant to help him, he said, "I can make it worth your time."

"What exactly do you have in mind?"

"You really want that donation for the hospital fund, don't you?"

She nodded. "Are you trying to say that you'll make a donation if I pick up your rental payments?"

He asked some questions about the hospital and the amount of money still needed. And for a moment, he was actually pleasant enough without a snarl or a nasty word. She answered all of his questions and waited.

He paused as though he were having second thoughts. Then with a deep sigh and a nod, he said, "I'll do it. Besides, I hate riding on that ferry, especially in the winter."

She resisted the urge to smile because this was too good to be true. With Blackwell, she knew there had to be a catch. "What aren't you saying?"

"So you aren't as naive as I thought. The deal is that you have to pick up the rent payments from all of my properties and if you don't, you'll relinquish your lease on the bookstore space."

She gaped at him. That was what he was after all along. He wanted her out so he could sell the building. They would tear down the old historic building to build some apartment complex. Housing on the island was getting hard to come by. Developers were always on the lookout for a location to build apartments or condos.

"You do want the donation, don't you?" His dark gaze probed her.

She wanted to tell him exactly what he could do with his deal and walk away, but her feet wouldn't cooperate. Her thoughts turned to her father and that scary night of his heart attack. What if it happened again? What if they didn't have time to transport him to the mainland?

And he wasn't the only one who would benefit from having a fully staffed hospital within minutes of their house. She couldn't live with herself if she walked away from this opportunity? After all, how hard could it be to pick up the rent payments?

"Yes, I do." But a little voice in the back of her mind said this offer was too good to be true. "What's the catch?"

"There's no catch. If you collect *all* of the payments, I'll make the donation."

Just to be sure he understood the large amount needed for the hospital, she told him the exact amount again. She noticed how the color in his face drained at the large dollar amount. "Are you still sure you want to make this deal?"

He nodded. "I am. And are you prepared to move out of the building if you fail?"

She leveled her shoulders. "I'm not going to fail. But I think we should put this in writing. I don't want either of us to confuse the terms we've just agreed to."

"Agreed."

She followed him to his office—she used the term loosely. The room she would guess had at one time been a dining room because there was a large crystal chandelier in the center of the room. She would guess that if it were cleaned, it might actually be pretty, but at this point it was layered in dust and cobwebs.

The rest of the room had an inch-thick layer of dust. Cobwebs hung in the corners of the room. They were big. And if the cobwebs were huge, she didn't even want to think about the size of the spiders that had spun them. A shiver raced down her spine. Her gaze moved to the floor, just to make sure there was nothing crawling toward her.

How in the world did this man live in this filth? It wasn't like he couldn't afford a cleaning staff? Or if he wanted to be cheap, he could run a vacuum just like everyone else. Maybe not now that he was on crutches, but those were recent and didn't explain all of the neglect.

His desk was covered in stacks of papers. In the center was an old adding machine. The white tape spilled out of it, over the mess of papers on the desk, and continued into a heap on the floor. *Yikes*!

She wouldn't classify herself as a clean freak but this place was giving her the heebie-jeebies. She couldn't wait to get out of there. She had no idea how Liam could stand to work there. The poor guy.

Blackwell held out a pen and paper to her. "Sign it."

She accepted them. When she turned the paper to read it, she was surprised to find his handwriting was legible. It spelled out the terms of their agreement and included the exact amount she'd quoted him for the hospital building.

Her gaze paused over the part about her relinquishing the bookshop—the shop where she had so many plans she intended to implement in the new year, starting with the reading nook in the front of the shop. Could she really bear to part with it?

Her chest tightened at the thought. She'd been a bookworm since she was a young child. She read everything and anything. As she grew up, she found herself more inclined to stay home and read a book than to join her friends on an adventure to the mainland for shopping.

But as much as she loved her bookshop, she loved her father more. He'd always been there for her—even believing in her bookshop dream so much that he'd invested in her business when she'd started it. She'd used the funds to build up her inventory. And within two years, she'd been able to pay him back every dollar.

Now he needed her to step up for him. And she wouldn't let him down. She gripped the pen and signed her name.

"It's done." She handed him the paper back. "Who do I need to collect payments from?"

He handed her what looked to be a green ledger sheet. He had scrawled out the list of names on the far-left side as well as their addresses. It was a long list. She suspected this man's wealth was far greater than any of the rumors alleged.

She turned and headed for the door. She could hear the clip-clop of him hobbling along behind her. Without pausing at the door, she rushed outside, anxious for a breath of fresh air.

As she made her way down the steps, Blackwell called out behind her. "Don't forget. If you fail to collect even one rent payment on that sheet, I get the bookshop."

She refused to let him see that his words heightened her worry. She still had a bad feeling there was something about this agreement she'd missed, but whatever it was, she'd overcome it. She would not fail, because absolutely everything she cared about was on the line.

Chapter Ten

"**Y**OU DID WHAT?"

Later that evening, Liam told himself that he couldn't have possibly heard Mel correctly. It was the only logical explanation because there was no way she'd make a deal with Blackwell. The man couldn't be trusted. He was only out to help one person—himself.

But this certainly wasn't the right setting to have a serious conversation. They were at the Apple Blossom Farm surrounded by people in holiday attire, from Santa hats to red, white, and green sweaters to scarves decorated with snowmen. They stood near a large fire pit with flames licking the evening sky. It was surrounded by cut tree trunks being used as seating. Not far away was a stand offering hot chocolate and cider as well as marshmallows for toasting.

The farm's pond was now frozen and turned into an informal ice-skating rink. Smiling people were all around them. He wanted to be one of those smiling people, but his concern for Mel subdued his good mood.

It was hard to hear over the holiday music blasting from large speakers and the people shouting to be heard over the music. And yet everyone appeared to be having a good time at the holiday skating party.

Even Mel was smiling. Why was she smiling? Didn't she realize the trouble she was in with Blackwell.

Her cheeks and the tip of her nose were pink from the cold. She looked totally adorable. He should let this thing go with Blackwell and just enjoy the evening. After all, it was rare for them to have some time to themselves, but he just couldn't let this go.

He had to warn Mel that she was making a mistake. She couldn't trust Blackwell to keep up his end of the deal. Did she honestly think Blackwell would part with his money?

He leaned near her and lowered his voice. "Mel, you have to get out of this deal with Blackwell. Tell him you made a mistake. Tell him whatever you want, but just end it."

"I can't." Her tone was very matter-of-fact.

"What do you mean you can't? Of course you can. I'll even go with you. We can go now."

She shook her head. "I need to do this."

"What exactly did you agree to?"

"You don't want to hear about that now. It's a beautiful evening, and we have skating to do."

He crossed his arms, refusing to budge. "I can't enjoy myself when I'm worried about you."

She sighed. "Fine. If you promise to skate with me, I'll tell you the deal."

He nodded. All the while he wondered why Blackwell had singled out Mel to make a deal. What did she have that he wanted?

"Stop frowning," Mel called out over a chorus of "Jingle Bells." "You don't want your face to freeze with that expression, do you?"

When the teasing smile returned to her face, it was hard for him to remain in a bad mood. "I'm just worried about you."

Her eyes filled with warmth. "Thanks. But you know that's not a one-way street. I worry about you too. And that's why I'm so happy you agreed to meet me here. It's been too long since we did something fun together. Now let's go skate."

He smiled and shook his head. "Same old Mel."

She pressed a hand to her hip. "What does that mean?"

"It means you're always the first to lead the charge. Okay. Let's go."

A few minutes later, they had their skates laced and made their way onto the ice. The pond was filled with happy skaters, from the youngsters just taking their first strides across the ice to the grandparents and even some great-grandparents. It was quite a successful turnout.

Next to him, Mel called out greetings to the other skaters. The worry had faded from her eyes, and she looked as though she were enjoying herself. When she slipped her hand into his, his breath hitched in the back of his throat.

Things between them never used to be complicated, but suddenly he felt awkward around her. Maybe that was because he'd been working up the courage to ask her out on a real date just before he'd gotten the horrific news about Audrey's sudden death. After that phone call, his life hadn't quite been his own. It had been all about doing what was best for his son.

He expelled a breath as he tried not to stare at Mel. He didn't want her to get uncomfortable around him, since she didn't show any interest in becoming romantically involved. And he didn't have the time to be a devoted boyfriend. His time was now filled with loads of laundry, sinks full of dishes, and bedtime stories. It was a juggling act, and he was struggling not to drop any of life's balls.

"Welcome, everyone." Charlie McQueen, owner of the Apple Blossom farm, came over the loudspeakers. "It's great to see you all here. Make sure you stop by the bonfire and toast some marshmallows, and there's warmed cider and hot chocolate to wet your whistle. And now it's time for a couple's skate. So find that special someone, and make your way to the ice."

Liam looked over at Mel to see if she was making her way off the ice, but instead he felt her gloved hand tighten her hold on him. It appeared they were doing the couple's skate. His heart beat faster.

His gaze lowered to where their hands were entwined. He swallowed hard. As much time as they spent together, he realized they barely ever touched. And yet her hand being in his felt so natural—so right.

He lifted his gaze to meet hers, but she wasn't looking in his direction. She was glancing around at all of the other couples crowding the skating area. And there were a lot, from couples who had been together close to fifty years to young kids who probably hadn't even had their first date. And then there was Mel and himself...

Nothing was implied by a couples skate. Right? Mel didn't mean anything by taking his hand—at least that was what he told himself.

As "It's The Most Wonderful Time of The Year" played, they made their way around the outer edge of the pond. He wanted to believe the words, but it just didn't feel right at this point. There was still so much to accomplish by Christmas.

Mel gently elbowed him. When he glanced at her, she asked, "Aren't you glad you came?"

He automatically gave her hand a squeeze. "Yes, I am."

He meant it. He really did enjoy spending time with her. There was just something about being around Mel that had him wanting to believe that anything was possible. But was that realistic?

She squeezed his hand back as she smiled, and the awkwardness he'd felt earlier faded away. Instead, a comforting warmth filled his chest and radiated outward.

When the song ended, he said, "How about some hot chocolate?"

"As long as we can toast some marshmallows."

"Sounds like a plan to me."

They made their way over and exited the pond. When Mel released his hand, he immediately missed her touch. Maybe he shouldn't have suggested the hot chocolate just yet. However, it was too late to take it back as Mel was already seated on a fallen tree trunk that was being used as a bench loosening the laces on her skates.

Once they both changed into their boots, they opted to get some refreshments. The line was long, but it moved quickly. While they waited, people came up to Mel and told her how excited they were for Bluestar's first Christmas bingo. Mel chatted with them and even sold a couple of tickets.

He listened while she explained that the ticket would get them two bingo cards as well as all of the popcorn and refreshments they wanted. He was proud of how much effort she'd put into the event.

They both picked out a couple of giant marshmallows to toast. Next to them were large woven baskets filled with twigs to hold the marshmallows over the fire.

As they sat next to the fire, he glanced over at Mel. She still had a big beautiful smile on her face. He worried that this deal with Blackwell was going to wipe the smile from her face, and that it wouldn't return.

"So, what is the exact deal you have with Blackwell?"

She told him about her brief meeting with Blackwell. The fact that she had risked her bookshop on this deal shocked him. He knew that she deeply loved the shop. She'd be lost without it. Would Blackwell really be so greedy that he'd make her a deal there was no chance she could win?

The answer was immediate and emphatic. Yes.

The problem with Mel was she wanted to see the good in people. She had been lucky not to have to deal with the likes of Blackwell. Liam hadn't been as fortunate. He knew that people only let them see what they wanted you to see, and when you peeled back the layers, sometimes a stranger lurked beneath.

It was what happened with Audrey. They'd so desperately wanted their relationship to work that they tried to make each other happy, even to the point of sacrificing their own happiness. An arrangement like that can only last so long, and theirs came to a sad conclusion—one they both knew was for the best.

He shoved away the memories. He could no longer help Audrey, but he could do his best to help Mel keep her beloved bookshop—if she'd let him. That was a *big* if because Mel was crazy independent. She preferred to be the one offering the help like she was doing for him by watching Tate and for her father, whom she'd been practically coddling since his heart attack. It was time for someone to watch out for her.

"Mel, can I ask you something?"

"Sure. What is it?"

"Are you really going to go through with this deal with Blackwell?"

She didn't hesitate when she nodded her head. "I signed an agreement." She studied him for a moment. "Stop worrying. How hard can this be? All I have to do is visit a bunch of businesses and rental properties to collect their rent, and then I'm done. And then the hospital will have the funding it needs to break ground."

"Let me help you."

Her brows rose. "Collect rent payments?"

He nodded. "We can split the list in half."

She shook her head. "I can handle it."

"What if it isn't as easy as you're imagining?"

"I'll deal with it. Stop worrying." She glanced back at her marshmallow. "Oh no." She quickly withdrew it from the bonfire and blew out the flames. The puffy white treat was now browned in places with just a couple of black marks. Mel blew on it a little more before she devoured it. A smile lifted the corners of her lips. "Delicious."

He loved seeing her so happy, and so he let his concerns drop. For now. There would be plenty of time to discuss her unwise deal with Blackwell when there weren't sweet treats and a free flow of smiles.

After finishing the hot chocolate and marshmallows, he found he didn't want the evening to end. "Would you like to skate a little more?"

Her gaze moved to where her skates rested on the ground near them. "I think I'm going to pass tonight. I'm a little tired."

A wave of disappointment washed over him. "Sure. I understand. We should get going."

They gathered their things, and in a companionable silence, they headed for the parking area. It had been a delightful evening. And he didn't say that lightly. He couldn't remember the last time he'd enjoyed himself so much. She was so easy to be with. He would have to make a point of doing things like this with her more often.

Just as they were leaving, Sara and Kent arrived. Sara's face lit up. "Hey, guys, where are you going?"

"We've already skated," Mel said. "And make sure you get some marshmallows to toast. They're good."

"Just don't catch yours on fire like someone we know." Liam's gaze moved to Mel as she rolled her eyes.

"Look up," Sara said.

"What?" He had no idea what his brother's girlfriend was talking about.

"Just look up."

And so he lifted his chin at the same time as Mel. They were standing beneath a black wrought iron arch. Above their heads the iron had been worked into the outline of an apple. Dangling from the arch was a sprig of green leaves with little white berries. It was attached to the arch by a red bow.

"It's mistletoe." There was a note of glee in Sara's voice.

Both of them looked at Sara and his brother, both of whom were grinning back at them. Surely they didn't actually expect them to kiss, did they? He wanted to tell them it was never going to happen...but then he glanced over at Mel at the same time she looked at him.

Mel didn't look upset by the idea. Did she want to kiss him? The thought of her being attracted to him did crazy things to his chest. Suddenly, his heart was beating erratically, and his breathing was coming in short gasps.

His gaze lowered to her lips. They were a rosy pink and beckoning for him to kiss them. But he couldn't—he shouldn't. They were friends. And a kiss... It might change things. He mentally listed all of the reasons he couldn't get involved with her or anyone at this point.

"Well, are you going to kiss her?" Kent looked expectantly at him.

He frowned at his brother. He'd have thought he'd be on his side and help calm down Sara, who seemed way too eager for them to kiss.

"Kiss!" *clap*

"Kiss!" *clap*

"Kiss!" *clap*

Suddenly, there was a small crowd of people standing around them continuing to cheer and clap.

Liam inwardly groaned. Could this get any worse? He looked to Mel for some direction. He noticed the pink in her cheeks. She was as uncomfortable with this public scene as him. Maybe it was best just to kiss and get this over with. After all, it was just a little kiss. No big deal. In a heartbeat it'd be over, and life could get back to normal.

Not thinking of the ramifications, he leaned toward her. He pressed his lips to hers. They were soft and surprisingly warm. His heart thudded against his ribs.

So this was what it was like to kiss Mel? It was even better than he'd imagined it to be. Way better. He deepened the kiss, and she followed him. He didn't want it to end. He could stay right here with her forever.

Mel pulled back. His eyes sprang open. He saw the confusion reflected in her eyes. Her cheeks were now stained a deep crimson red, but she wasn't smiling at him.

Oh no. Was she upset with him? He didn't get a chance to ask as an applause went up around them.

"I've got to go." Mel rushed off to where they'd parked their carts.

He looked at his brother, who was still smiling. "What did you go and do that for?"

"Because if I leave it up to you and her, you two will never figure out that you belong together. You two are the only ones who don't seem to notice that you're perfect for each other."

He couldn't believe his own brother had said that to him. *Wait*. People actually thought he and Mel would make a good couple? Who were these people? And why were they talking about Mel and him?

Before he could form a coherent question, Sara and his brother moved off, leaving Liam alone with his troubling thoughts. His gaze moved in the direction of Mel's cart. They should talk. But as his eyes scanned the distance, he found she was gone. Maybe it was for the best. With a little time to calm down, maybe they could just pretend the kiss never happened. But was that what he really wanted?

CHAPTER ELEVEN

8 days until Christmas

CHRISTMAS FESTIVITIES WERE IN full-swing.

Merry shoppers were out and about, searching for the perfect Christmas gift.

Normally, all of this hubbub would excite Melinda, but not today. Even though she had Ava working in the bookshop, she still didn't have a chance to slip away. Not even to pick up her lunch or to call her father and check in on him.

And it didn't help that she hadn't slept well the night before. Every time she closed her eyes, Liam was there kissing her. Even the memory of the kiss made her heart pitter-patter.

What had he been thinking to kiss her in front of all of those people? He might as well have taken a photo of the kiss and posted it on social media because it felt as though everyone in Bluestar now knew about it. And trying to explain that the mistletoe kiss hadn't meant anything had fallen on deaf ears. People appeared certain that she and Liam were a couple. Nothing could be further from the truth.

And then there was the deal she'd made with Blackwell. She hadn't admitted it to Liam, but she was worried. She still hadn't figured out the catch, but knowing Blackwell, the deal was slanted in his direction. The sooner she started collecting the rent, the sooner she'd learn about the challenge ahead of her. Whatever it was, she'd overcome it because there was no way she was parting with the bookshop or her plan for a hospital.

"Melinda? Yoohoo. Melinda, did you hear me?"

She turned to see Ava standing on the other side of the counter. Ava had a puzzled look on her face. Melinda had totally been lost in her thoughts.

"What did you say?"

"I said if you want to slip out, now is your chance. The puppet show is about to begin, and things have quieted down."

Melinda looked around the shop and realized she was right. Most of the people were squeezed into the front, where she'd cleared out a spot for the puppet stage, and colorful plastic chairs lined up for the children. The parents were either browsing through the nearby bookshelves or lined up in the back, holding their children's coats.

She glanced back at Ava. "Are you sure?"

"Go. I've got it covered." She moved to the cash register. "And grab a late lunch or early dinner while you're out."

Melinda was hesitant to go. She really hated being gone in case there was another rush. But Ava was right. She needed to get going if she was going to keep up her end of the deal with Blackwell.

"Thank you. I'll have my phone on me, so if things get busy, just call me. I'll come right back."

"Stop worrying," Ava said. "I know what I'm doing."

Melinda smiled and nodded. "Yes, you do. Thank you."

"Let me know if there's anything else I can do to help. After all, this hospital is for everyone on the island. You shouldn't have to shoulder so much of the work for it."

It was true. This was going to be a fully functioning community hospital with as many bells and whistles as their budget could accommodate. She couldn't think of a better Christmas present for the islanders. Even Blackwell was swayed now that he'd broken his ankle and realized what a pain it was to commute to the mainland for appointments.

She rushed to the back to grab her coat. It wasn't snowing at the moment, but it was still cold and blustery. Wrapped in her coat and a red scarf with white snowmen printed on it, she rushed out the door with the list of renters in hand.

Her first stop was Beach Love Yoga. The cute studio wasn't as busy as it was in the summer, but Melinda spotted more than a dozen people in a yoga session.

She was just about to step up to the reception desk to ask for the owner, Summer Turner, when she emerged from a back hallway. As soon as she spotted Melinda, a smile lit up her face.

They'd known each other most of their lives as they both grew up on Bluestar Island. Melinda was thankful the first name on the list was a friend.

Summer approached her. "Hi. I haven't seen you here lately."

"I'm sorry about that. I've been meaning to start my classes again, but I've been really busy with my father."

A look of concern came over her face. "How's he doing?"

"Good. Just trying to get him to stay away from the pizza and fried food has been a challenge.

"Old habits are hard to break, but I'm glad to hear that he's doing well. He really had us worried."

"Tell me about it. Those were some really long days in the hospital. I hope we never have to go through that again."

"I heard you had some company in the hospital."

For a moment, Melinda wasn't sure who Summer was referring to because a lot of Bluestar residents made a point of visiting her father when he was in the hospital. It was so sweet of them. Even Birdie Neill made the trip to the mainland.

But then it dawned on Melinda who Summer was referring to, Liam. Everyone was certain they were dating, but nothing could have been further from the truth. Liam had just stepped up as a friend. Being a paramedic, he had been on the call for her father, and then he'd stuck around to help her out because she'd been losing her mind when things were touch and go with her father.

However, the mistletoe kiss will undoubtedly resurrect all of those rumors.

"Liam was a huge help." She hoped Summer would let that particular subject drop right there.

"I heard about your kiss last night." Summer sent her a knowing smile. "Does this mean you're officially dating?"

"No! We're just friends."

Summer sighed. "Sorry. I just heard you've had Tate at the bookshop this week, and then with what happened last night, the town is already talking about your wedding."

Melinda inwardly groaned. "Liam needed a babysitter because the daycare is shorthanded right now, and I offered to help out." Not wanting to talk more about her relationship with Liam, she decided to turn the conversation around. "So, how are you and Greg doing?"

Immediately Summer's face lit up. "We are great. For a long time, I didn't think we were meant to be. And just when I was about to give up hope, we found our way to each other. Now we couldn't be happier."

"I'm so happy for both of you."

"Thanks. So, if you aren't here to take a class, you must be here to collect a donation for the hospital fund."

Melinda once more shook her head. "Actually, I'm not. I know you've already contributed, and I want to thank you. It means a lot."

Summer's brows drew together. "If you don't want to take a class and you aren't looking for a donation, what has you visiting me today?"

"Actually, I'm here to pick up your rent payment."

Summer's brows rose high on her forehead and then settled into a dark line. The light in her eyes dimmed. "Are you serious? You're working for cranky Blackwell?"

Melinda had a feeling this was going to be the reaction she garnered from most, if not all, of the people on the list. "Not exactly."

"I can't believe this. How did he get you to go over to the dark side?"

Melinda resisted the urge to laugh. "Laying it on a little thick, aren't you?"

Summer shook her head. "No. That man is awful. He doesn't have one nice word to say about anyone. He's only interested in his money, and to make matters worse, he's going around the island jacking up the rent on people who can't afford it." Summer crossed her arms. "Why are you doing this?"

Melinda explained about the town council's ultimatum, Blackwell's injury, and her deal with him to fund the hospital. She had a feeling she would be doing a lot of explaining between now and when she picked up the last rent check. "So, this is the one and only time I'll be picking up your rent payment."

Summer's gaze searched hers. "You know it's never going to happen, don't you?"

"What?"

"Him donating money for the hospital. He'll never part with it. Not a chance. I bet he has heaps of cash in a giant safe. He probably sits around all day counting it."

Melinda could actually envision him doing exactly that as he sat at his giant oak desk. "He must be so lonely."

"Who? Blackwell?" When Melinda nodded, Summer said, "He only has himself to blame. Who would want to spend time with him? He's so...so grinchy."

"I wonder what happened to him. No one is that miserable naturally."

"I have no idea. Let me get the check for you." Summer moved to the reception desk and retrieved a white envelope with Blackwell's name on it.

When she handed it over, Melinda said, "Thank you. I hope you can understand why I'm doing this."

"I do. I'm sorry I jumped to the wrong conclusion. I was just so shocked. I'm sure I won't be the only one. I'm not so sure you're going to receive welcome greetings from the other businesses."

"I suppose not." She worried her bottom lip. She didn't like conflict or upsetting people. "Trust me. I'll never do this ever again."

"Be careful. The man can't be trusted. I just know there's some sort of loophole in the agreement."

"Thanks. Liam warned me too. I just have to believe after his accident that he sees things different now."

"I guess so." There was disbelief in her voice. "Hey. Are you going to the play at the school tonight?"

Truthfully, she hadn't planned on going to the play, but she could tell by the way Summer had asked that she needed something. "What do you need?"

"Well, Pam Wilson's daughter came down with the bug that's going around. Anyway, Pam was going to help with the stage crew. You know, moving the setting around and working the curtain. And now I'm left finding someone to help me at the last minute."

Melinda thought of the Christmas cards she had to finish in order to drop them in the mail the next day and the presents she needed to wrap. Just as quickly as the thoughts came to her, she dismissed them. "I'd be happy to help you."

A look of relief came over Summer's face, followed by a smile. "Thank you so much. If you can be there by six, I'll show you what needs to be done."

"Okay. I'll see you then."

"I really appreciate this. I hope you aren't working too hard. You don't want to miss the holiday festivities."

Immediately, her thoughts rewound to her skating with Liam the night before. She'd had a fantastic time, right up until the point where he kissed her. Actually, it wasn't the kiss. It had been toe-curling fantastic. It was the confusion she now felt. Was Liam telling her he wanted to take their relationship to the next level? And if he did, what was she supposed to say or do?

Summer said she had to get to a class and moved on. Melinda opened the envelope and checked that the amount on the check was the same as that on her list. It was. She placed the check in her purse for safekeeping and then checked the payment off her list. One down, no make that two payments down. She checked off her own payment that she'd already given Blackwell.

She stopped at two other businesses. At both places, they were none too happy to hear she was doing Blackwell's bidding. They didn't give her a hard time. It was just that all of the pleasantness evaporated as soon as she mentioned Blackwell's name. From that point forward, it was all business and nothing more.

This agreement was going to be harder than she'd allowed herself to believe. She didn't like when people she'd known all of her life frowned at her and showed disdain where she was concerned. The sooner she got this job completed, the better. It was certainly taking the jolly out of her holiday.

And she needed to talk to Liam. The sooner they straightened things out between them, the better.

CHAPTER TWELVE

H E WAS RUNNING LATE.

Liam finished up his work at the Blackwell mansion. He glanced around, hoping to spot Blackwell, but the man was nowhere in sight. Blackwell was usually peering over Liam's shoulder and pointing out ways he could do his job better.

Tonight was the big Christmas play, so he had to leave Blackwell's a little early. He had to be at the school in case there were any problems with the set. It seemed simple enough.

Liam worked through his lunch break so he could leave early that day. He wanted to check on Tate before he headed over to the school auditorium. There were always last-minute tweaks that needed to be tended to.

Luckily for him, Jack had some free time today and was able to take Tate for him. He never imagined months ago when he'd volunteered to help with the set for the school play that his life would end up being so chaotic, but he supposed this was good practice for when Tate was in school.

After stopping by his brother's place and finding Tate asleep on the couch, he thanked his brother again and made a quick exit. He headed over to the school. There was already a buzz of activity as everyone got ready for the performance.

Liam moved the fireplace to the center of the stage. Tonight's rendition was *The Night Before Christmas*. He'd caught bits and pieces of the play, but he was looking forward to seeing the entire production. He knew how hard the kids had worked on learning their parts. It felt like a lifetime since he'd been one of those kids up on the stage. He'd been a nervous wreck when he'd had to do the Christmas play. He definitely wasn't cut out to be an actor. He was much more comfortable with a hammer in one hand and sandpaper in the other.

"It looks great!"

He turned to find Aster and Sam Bell. Aster looked as though she were about to give birth at any moment. He remembered when Audrey was that far along with Tate. She couldn't wait to give birth. And he'd been scared because he'd felt so out of his element and had no idea how to help her.

From the start, Audrey always seemed to know what to do where their son was concerned. Him, not so much. And now he was on his own. There wasn't a day that passed when at some point in the day he didn't feel adequate when it came to Tate, but he just kept trying to do his best and hoped it was enough.

Aster and Sam stood there admiring the artificial Christmas tree. It had been the easiest part of the set. He merely took it out of the box and assembled it. The fireplace had to be cut from plywood and assembled before being painted to look like it was made of red bricks.

"It did turn out really well."

"We're lucky you volunteered." Aster smiled at him while her hand pressed to the small of her back. "You did an amazing job."

"I didn't do all of this alone. I had help from a few seniors."

Aster nodded her head. "You all did a fantastic job."

Sam and Aster's daughter came rushing up to them in a mouse costume. "How do I look?"

"Adorable," Aster said.

All three of them oohed and aahed over her. She looked cute with a long gray tail and big round ears with pink centers, as well as long whiskers from her rounded nose.

Liam was certain this year's play was going to be the best one yet. He hoped that Mel wouldn't miss it. He glanced around the auditorium but didn't see her. He should have said something to her before now, but he didn't know what to say. And he noticed she hadn't exactly reached out to talk to him. What did that say about their kiss?

"Hey, Liam, can we move the Christmas tree a little to the right?" The director's voice drew him from his thoughts.

"Sure. No problem." As he turned, he spotted Mel standing backstage, speaking with Summer Turner.

He wanted to go over and say hello, but when his gaze met the director's, there was a look of urgency on the woman's face. He started toward the tree and by the time he positioned it in just the right spot, which took a number of attempts, Mel had disappeared from sight.

The lights had dimmed, and it was showtime.

Liam didn't have a seat for the play, so he moved to the back of the auditorium. He wasn't surprised to find it was standing room only. His gaze moved over the crowd, searching for Mel. In the dim lighting, he had trouble finding her, but he was certain she was somewhere in the large crowd.

He leaned against a support post and watched the play. For elementary school students, it was pretty good. He could easily imagine clapping for his son one day not so far into the future.

The curtain closed to rousing applause. When the curtain opened again, all of the actors were lined up, and there was a standing ovation. Liam joined in the applause. Those kids certainly deserved it.

When the curtain closed again, the lights came up in the auditorium. He needed to make it backstage to help with the clean-up, but at the moment there was nowhere for him to go as the large crowd streamed toward him and out of the auditorium.

He said hello to passersby and nodded his head to others. It seemed like he knew everyone in attendance. It was what happened in small towns. And he noticed a lot of the people he'd graduated with had little ones of their own.

When at last he could make it backstage, he turned the corner and nearly ran into Mel. He stepped back. "Hey, there you are."

Her gaze avoided his. "Were you looking for me?"

"Um...no... Um... I mean I saw you backstage before the play, but then I lost track of you."

She nodded. "I was helping with the stage crew. Pam's daughter has the bug that's going around, so she wasn't able to make it. So I filled in."

"That was nice of you."

She shrugged. Her gaze still didn't meet his. "That's what we do in Bluestar—help each other out. I didn't do anything you wouldn't have done."

He had to fix this. It was obvious the kiss had been a big mistake. If he didn't fix things with her now—so she would actually look at him again—he feared their friendship would be forever damaged.

"Mel, hey, um...I've been meaning to talk to you. I...um, need to apologize to you about the kiss."

Her gaze lifted to meet his. "Everyone in town is talking about it. They're even talking about us getting married."

He raked his fingers through his hair. "I never thought it would blow up like this. Did you tell them nothing is going on between us? It was just an innocent kiss to stop them from chanting at us."

Her gaze searched his. "And that's the only reason you, um...kissed me?"

He got the feeling there was no right answer to that question. No matter what he said, he would be in trouble. He just wanted to go back in time and undo it.

As soon as the thought came to him, he knew it wasn't the truth. That kiss had stirred something within him. It made him wish their circumstances were less complicated, and then maybe they could explore that kiss some more. But now wasn't the time for that. He just needed to get their friendship back on track.

"Yes. That's it." He couldn't read the expression on her face. "Can we go back to being friends and ignore the gossip?"

She didn't answer right away, making him worry. Had he done irreparable harm to their friendship?

"Yes." She nodded. "Of course. It was no big deal."

Really? He wasn't sure how he felt about her brushing off his kiss.

Summer joined them on the stage. "Some of us are going out for a late dinner. Do you guys want to join us?"

"Thanks," Liam said. "But I need to pick up Tate and head home."

All eyes turned to Mel. "And I've got to check on my dad before heading home."

"You two are no fun. But I want to thank you both for all you did to make tonight's production the best." After a little more chatting about the play and the children, Summer made her exit.

"Are you ready to go?" Liam asked.

"I am. I just need to grab my stuff."

"I'll wait. We can leave together."

"I'd like that."

When they made their way through the auditorium, there were still a number of people standing around. As heads turned in their direction, the conversation dwindled off.

Agnes Dewey stepped into their path. She stood between them and the door. Her brows were drawn together as her lips puckered as though she'd just finished sucking on a lemon.

"How could you do it?" Agnes stared straight at Mel.

"Excuse me?" Mel's eyes filled with confusion.

"Don't act all innocent. The whole town knows you're now Blackwell's henchman."

Color rushed to Mel's cheeks. "I am not."

Agnes's eyes narrowed. "Don't try to deny it. We heard you've already been to Hamming It Up, TJ's Boat Shop, and Beach Love Yoga."

Just then Dorothy Bellman marched up to them. Hostility radiated from her. "Shame on you." She reached into her purse and pulled out a white envelope. She held it out to Mel. "Don't bother coming to my store. Here's your money, including the rent increase. Shame on you."

"Hey!" Liam stiffened. "There's no need to speak to Mel that way."

Dorothy's narrowed gaze settled on him. "Of course you'd stick up for her. You've already gone to the dark side by agreeing to work for that—that curmudgeon."

He knew his choice to take the job wasn't a popular one with the locals. Horace Blackwell had done nothing in recent years but alienate everybody in Bluestar, but what people didn't stop to consider was that when Liam became a full-time father, he couldn't be as choosy about his work. They needed money.

"Since you don't know all of the facts"—Liam struggled to keep his tone neutral—"you can't judge other people's choices."

"Hmpff..." Dorothy crossed her arms. "What I know is that Blackwell raised my rent twenty-five percent. Twenty-five. That's highway robbery. How am I supposed to pay that every month? Especially in the winter months."

"Mine went up too," someone in the background called out.

Mel stepped forward. "I'm sorry. I didn't mean to upset you all when I made the deal with Blackwell. I was trying to do something to help the community."

"You have a funny way of showing it." Without another word, the woman turned on her heel and marched out the door.

Mel was left standing there with her mouth gaping. Liam felt bad for her. He knew aligning herself with Blackwell, even for the purest of motives, would be bad. He hadn't thought it would be this bad.

Agnes clucked her tongue and shook her head as she walked away.

Mel's throat bobbed as she swallowed. "It wasn't supposed to be like this." She turned to the small crowd of people staring at her. "I'm not aligned with him. I'm not. We made a deal so he'd help with the hospital."

The people turned away. Many of them headed out the door.

Even sweet Birdie Neill gave Mel an unhappy look. "Oh, dear, what have you done?"

Mel gasped.

But before Birdie could say more or Mel could defend her action, Birdie was surrounded by people. The conversation that had barely even started was cut off on an ominous note. They ushered Birdie out the door.

He turned to Mel. The color had drained from her face, leaving her complexion a pasty white. Her beautiful eyes reflected the pain she was experiencing.

Sympathy welled up in him. This outward hostility was very uncommon in Bluestar. He felt helpless, not knowing how to fix this for her. He was certain she was the target of misplaced frustration. And with Blackwell housebound, they couldn't voice their anger over his outrageous rent hikes to his face, and instead they took it out on Mel.

In that moment, he instinctively reached out to her. When she didn't move, he gently drew her closer until he was hugging her. "It'll be okay."

"No, it won't." Her voice was faint, but the anguish was unmistakable.

After that she didn't say anything. She stood there as though she were shocked by the reactions. The pain showed in her eyes.

"Are you ready to go?" he asked.

She nodded.

As they headed out the door into the inky black night, Liam kept thinking about Mel's deal with Blackwell. The man could be underhanded when it suited him, and poor Mel only ever wanted to see the best in people. This time her optimistic view of the world was going to cost her—maybe in the end it would cost her more than the loss of her bookshop. The thought weighed on him.

CHAPTER THIRTEEN

7 days before Christmas

E VERYTHING WOULD BE ALL right.

Melinda told herself that over and over again as she laid in bed, watching the sun coming up. Yesterday had been such a horrible day. Even things with Liam were a mess. Sure he'd apologized for kissing her and creating a firestorm of gossip. The part she hadn't expected was her utter disappointment when he dismissed the mistletoe kiss as though it truly didn't matter to him.

An internal war waged within her. Her mind insisted his dismissal of the kiss was for the best. Her heart wasn't up for the risks that came with love. And she didn't want to risk her special friendship with Liam.

Even though he'd tried to patch up their friendship, she wondered if they could go back to their easy-going closeness they'd had before the kiss. Or had that one spontaneous action permanently changed everything between them?

Unable to decide on an answer, she shifted her thoughts to her deal with Blackwell. She'd been certain it was the answer to funding the new hospital. She knew there would be a catch, but she had no idea she'd face such hostility from the people she called friends.

She vividly recalled Birdie's look of disapproval. It took a lot to upset Birdie. She was like a grandmother to so many on the island. She was always there with an encouraging word or compliment. Melinda had gotten neither of those last night.

She lay there in her full-size bed, snuggled under the comforter. The air around her was cool, and the covers felt so soft and comforting. She wanted to stay there all day. It was so much more appealing than getting out of bed and seeing the disappointment on everyone's faces.

Maybe the reactions were due to the initial shock of finding out she was helping Blackwell. Maybe now that they'd had the night to adjust to the idea, her friends would give her the benefit of the doubt. She would never knowingly do anything to hurt them. Surely they knew that. Didn't they?

When her alarm went off, she threw back the blankets. The chill in the morning air woke her up better than a dark cup of coffee. She ran her hands up her arms, which were covered in goosebumps. She grabbed her fuzzy aqua robe and wrapped it tightly around herself.

She quickly moved through her morning routine. She skipped breakfast because she didn't have an appetite. And then she headed out the door.

She was happy to find no new snow to shovel and the sun shining. It would, hopefully, mean they'd have a huge crowd for that night's Christmas bingo. It was the last hospital fundraiser she had planned for the year. Depending on how things worked out with Blackwell, it might be the last fundraiser. Period.

When she reached the bookshop, she unlocked the door and turned on the lights. It was time to prepare for one of the busiest days of the year, as there were only seven days until Christmas. And if prior years were an indication, the books would be flying off the shelves. And it was exactly what she needed if she was going to make her increased rent in the New Year.

As the morning wore on, Melinda grew concerned. The bookshop was eerily quiet. She kept telling herself that people were staying in bed a little later because it was such a cold morning. But as the clock moved from nine to ten and then to eleven, she knew something was definitely wrong.

She turned to Ava. "Does everyone know about what happened after the play last night?"

Ava didn't meet her gaze. Her only reply was a shrug.

Ava was a really nice young woman. She never had a bad word to say about anyone. And so Melinda knew Ava wasn't about to say something she thought might hurt her.

"It's okay, Ava. You can tell me. What's going on?"

Ava wrung her hands. "Um… They aren't coming."

"Who?" Surely she didn't mean the whole town. If that were the case, she might not have to worry about her deal with Blackwell—the lack of Christmas business would put her business in jeopardy.

"They were talking…"

"Who?"

Ava shrugged. "People."

Melinda reached out and gently touched Ava's shoulder. "Please talk to me. I need to know what's going on."

Ava hesitantly met Melinda's gaze.

"It's okay. Whatever it is, you can tell me. I promise I won't be upset with you."

"Well… Um… I heard after the fact that there was this impromptu meeting last night at the Lighthouse Café. People were upset you…um, sided with Blackwell."

"What?" She couldn't believe her ears. How could the people she'd known all of her life believe this of her. "I never sided with him about anything."

"I think they're hurt because many of them are struggling to make the increased rent."

"But don't they understand that I had nothing to do with the rent increase? I only agreed to do this to get the money for the hospital."

"Maybe you should tell them."

"I didn't think I'd have to explain I only had the best of intentions. These people that are upset are people I've known my whole life."

Still, Ava did have a good point. She needed to explain things. But she just couldn't bear telling the same story over and over again. It would take her forever, and she didn't have time to waste—especially if the town was going to boycott the bookshop.

She glanced around at the empty aisles, empty chairs, and the checkout counter, where she'd spent countless hours chatting with people who were practically family. The sting of their outrage tore at her heart. She blinked repeatedly. She would not give into the tears that threatened to fall.

She didn't have time to feel sorry for herself. She had to fix this problem. There had to be a way to get through to them that she would never do anything to intentionally hurt them. If anything, she wanted to protect them.

She glanced at the clock behind the checkout counter. It was almost lunchtime. A lot of people would crowd into the Lighthouse Café for some of the steaming hot vegetable soup and homemade bread.

She turned to Ava. "Will you be okay here while I step out for a little bit?"

Ava glanced around at the empty store. "I think I can handle things here. What are you going to do?"

"Why do you think I'm going to do anything?"

"Because you have that determined look in your eyes. When you look like that, it's because you have a plan in mind."

A little smile pulled at the corner of Melinda's lips. "I hadn't realized you knew me so well."

"We work together almost every day. I know you. And I know you'd never hurt anyone. I think they're just in shock that you would strike a deal with Blackwell. Once they calm down, they'll realize you have good intentions."

"Maybe I should have you go speak to them for me."

"I... I would, if you think it'll help."

"Thank you." Melinda knew Ava wasn't comfortable speaking in front of a crowd, besides this wasn't her fight. "I appreciate it more than you know. But this is my problem. I'll fix it. Or at least I'll give it my best attempt." She rushed to the office and grabbed her scarf and coat. "I'll be back."

The sun was shining brightly and reflecting off the snow. Melinda reached into her pocket and retrieved her sunglasses. Normally, she'd walk to the café and enjoy the sunshine, but she didn't have time to waste. She had to tell them her side of the story before even more islanders made up their mind that she'd gone over to the dark side.

She rushed to her golf cart and tramped the accelerator. The cart slid on the icy road. Her fingers tightened on the steering wheel as she struggled to retain control. At the same time, she let up on the accelerator. At this rate, she might have been better off walking.

With a sigh, she cautiously made her way to the café. There wasn't any parking in front of the restaurant. Just as she predicted, it was a large crowd. Farther down the block, she found a spot and squeezed her cart into it.

She climbed out of the cart and set off toward the café. She was determined to nip this misunderstanding in the bud. She had to believe these people, who had been a part of her life as far back as she could remember, would understand and let go of this hostility.

The more she thought about how everyone had jumped to the wrong conclusion, the quicker her footsteps came. Lucky for her the sidewalk had been cleared, and the sun was doing its best to melt the rest.

She opened the door and stepped inside. The hubbub of conversations could be heard in the vestibule. Good. She wanted the largest crowd possible. And if she were lucky, there would be some of the town gossips. They would help her to get the word out that she wasn't fully involved with Blackwell and his nefarious schemes.

When she stepped into the dining room, she noticed the people dressed in their colorful Christmas sweaters. A number of them glanced at her before turning away. A moment later, they once more looked in her direction. Eyes widened. Hands covered mouths as they talked about her. Table by table a hush fell over the room.

Melinda's heart thudded in her chest. She had never been the center of a Bluestar scandal, and so this reaction made her very uncomfortable. She could feel the unwavering stares follow her to the long counter at the back of the café.

The only sounds were the ones coming from the kitchen. Apparently they were too busy cooking to notice what was going on in the dining room. That was okay. There were certainly enough people out here to hear her words and hopefully spread it around town.

As she walked, her mouth grew dry and her palms became damp. Public speaking was never one of her favorite classes in school. It appeared the passage of time hadn't changed things for her.

She stopped next to the back counter and turned. People strained their necks to see her. What were they expecting her to say? It didn't matter. She only had the truth to share with them.

She resisted the urge to swipe her palms over her jeans. Instead, she pulled down the zipper on her coat. *Wow! It's warm in here.*

She swallowed hard and willed her voice not to waver. "I have a few things to say."

"We can't hear you in the back!" called out a male voice.

She cleared her throat and then raised her voice. "I have a few things to say."

She paused. No one said anything. It appeared they could all hear her now. She glanced over at one table where someone was holding up a cell phone. Were they filming her?

Heat swirled in her chest and rushed to her cheeks. She'd been so worked up she hadn't even thought of her appearance, but it was too late for any of that not. She just needed to get this over with.

"I know you have all heard that I'm now working for Horace Blackwell. And a lot of you are upset with him for raising the rent. I want you to know a couple of things. First, I am not working for him. And second, I have nothing to do with the rent increase. It's going to affect me too."

A murmur rolled over the crowd. In the background, even the kitchen had grown quiet. Who knew her words could draw so much attention?

"Then why are you picking up the rent for him?" Agnes Dewey called out.

"Because I struck a deal with Mr. Blackwell."

Her words were cut off with a chorus of "I told you so." The voices grew louder and louder. Melinda's body tensed. Maybe this was a mistake. No one was listening to her.

A loud whistle echoed through the café. Birdie stood at a nearby table. As she lowered her hand to her side, she turned back to Melinda. "You were saying?"

Thank goodness for Birdie. At least she was willing to hear her out before casting her sentence. If only the rest of her neighbors and friends would give her the same courtesy.

Melinda's mouth was dry like the Sierra. She really wished she had a drink of water, but she pushed on. "I made a deal with Blackwell because it's the only way to make the new hospital a reality." Another murmur ran through the crowd. "I'm not sure if you're aware but the newly elected town council doesn't think trying to build a small hospital in Bluestar is possible. But Aster Bell convinced them to give me until the New Year to secure the rest of the funding. Otherwise, they're going to take the money you've all so graciously donated and use it for other purposes."

"What's wrong with that?"

Melinda remained quiet until the people stopped shouting. She wasn't going to get into an argument with them. It would only make matters worse. And they were plenty mad right now.

This time all it took was Birdie getting to her feet for people to shush up.

"Expanding the medical center would be nice, but it would still mean for more serious injuries that the person would have to wait to be transported to the mainland for more invasive testing and treatment. By having our own hospital, it would cut down that time considerably and lessen the time for complications."

"You just want this because of your father!"

She couldn't deny that, nor would she. "It's true. It's what gave me the initial idea. But the more I thought about what a small hospital and a full-time staff could offer our growing island, the more I realized it is what we need. It doesn't just have to be for emergency medicine. It could also play a part in preventive medicine. How many of you travel regularly to the mainland for doctor appointments?" When no one raised their hand, she said, "Come on. Raise your hand."

Five hands raised.

Five people. That's not many. She had to try harder. "If you didn't have to catch the ferry to the mainland and then arrange for transportation from the dock to the doctor's office, how much more likely would you be to go for that appointment?"

"But we go to the medical center."

"Right. For urgent treatment but not regular health screenings. With a hospital staff, it would be possible to reduce heart attacks and strokes. Cancer screenings would be available."

"Okay. We get it. But what does this have to do with you working for Blackwell?"

And so they'd come full circle.

"I saw an opportunity to help not only my father but the entire community. I agreed to pick up the rent payments if he would donate a large sum to the hospital building fund. It's what we need to keep this project on track."

"And he agreed?" Disbelief rang out loud and clear.

"It took some back and forth, but yes, he agreed."

"What's the catch?"

She drew in a deep breath and blew it out as she figured out how best to word her answer. "The catch is I have to collect every single rent. I can't be a dollar short or the deal is off. And I have to deliver all of the funds by Christmas Eve."

She left out the part about putting the bookshop on the line. She didn't want to make this arrangement about her. This hospital was all about the community. Now she needed the community behind her plan.

CHAPTER FOURTEEN

IT WAS TIME FOR Christmas Bingo.

With it being Saturday, Liam hadn't had to go to work at Blackwell's. Instead he'd done some housework, played with Tate, and then they'd gone to his woodshop. While Tate curled up in a chair and watched some cartoons on a digital tablet, Liam had worked on a very special Christmas present for Melinda.

He'd been working on it for months. It was a bookshelf, but it wasn't just any shelf. He'd taken the time to carve a design into it. He didn't have the money to buy presents for anyone this year except for Tate. So, he'd set out to make some gifts. He just hoped it turned out well.

Buzz.

He was just about to scoop up Tate and head to Jack's place. He glanced at the caller ID. He was surprised to see it was from Madison St. Claire, one of Bluestar's real estate agents. Could this be a lead on a house?

He pressed the phone to his ear. "Hello."

"Hey, Liam, I wanted to let you know that I have a three-bedroom house that is about to hit the market. I think you'll really like this place."

"Wow. That's fantastic. How much are they asking?"

Madison mentioned a number that landed near the top of his budget, but it was still in the realm of possibilities. "Has anything changed with your finances since we ran your prequalification for a mortgage?"

His pulse picked up its pace. This was the news he'd been waiting to hear. "No. Nothing has changed. How soon can I see it?"

"I'm hoping to get you in to view it before anyone else. I don't have the details yet, but I'll be in touch shortly."

Hope swelled in his chest. "Thank you."

"I hope this all works out. It'll be perfect for you and your son. Tate is going to love the fenced-in backyard."

Liam couldn't believe at last this was happening. This was the closest he'd come to buying a house. This past summer they'd sold before he even got a chance to view them, but with the lull of winter and Madison's help, this might actually happen.

A short time later, he stopped at Jack's place to drop off Tate. His brother was a really good sport about helping out with Tate, which totally surprised Liam. He didn't have to cajole or bribe his brother to watch Tate. In fact, Jack was the one to approach him. Since when was his brother into kids?

Liam didn't usually need this much help with Tate, but the lead up to Christmas was a busy one, and Melinda had asked him to help with bingo long before he became a full-time father. And there wasn't a chance he was going to let her down.

"Hey, Liam, do you want something to drink?" Jack asked.

"Sorry. I can't stay. I'm already a little late."

"Before you go, did you hear about what happened at the Lighthouse Café earlier today? I heard it was really quite a scene."

Liam shook his head. The café was always at the heart of the community. And if something happened, it didn't surprise him that it took place there. The part that did surprise him was that his brother listened to the gossip swirling around the town.

Liam helped Tate take his coat off. "I didn't, but you'll have to fill me in later. I've got to run." He held out a tote to his brother. "I packed some of his favorite toys and a couple of books. Do you have any questions?"

Jack shook his head. "We'll be good, won't we, Tate?"

Tate didn't respond. He was too busy driving a fire truck over the floor.

Liam glanced at his brother. "Thanks for doing this. I really appreciate it."

"No problem. I didn't have any other plans."

"Hey, Tate, come here." Liam knelt down and held out his arms to his son. When Tate ran into his father's embrace, he hugged him. "I've got to go, but be good for Uncle Jack. I'll be back soon. I love you."

"Wuv you."

And then Liam was out the door. He could imagine this really large crowd at the Bluestar Hall otherwise known as the island's community center. Mel would be rushing around trying to manage everything on her own. She didn't like to impose on people and usually tried to shoulder everything on her own.

He climbed into his cart and started the heater. As he drove through town, he couldn't help but notice all of the houses that were decorated in shades of red, white, and green. There were Santas in all sizes as well as some reindeer and a Santa's sleigh. The people of Bluestar went all out for the holidays.

He wondered when he bought a house, if Tate would expect him to decorate like so many of their neighbors. Probably. Luckily, Tate was too young to have such expectations. As it was, Liam hadn't even put up a Christmas tree. He figured he'd just take his presents for Tate over to his parents' house and put them under their tree. It'd be so much easier that way.

As he drew close to the community center, he was surprised by the availability of parking. He wheeled into a spot right in front and got out. He glanced around, surprised to find the place wasn't crowded.

Maybe people figured that parking would be a problem and decided to walk. And since it hadn't snowed that day, the sidewalks weren't bad. It made sense. Because everyone was excited about Christmas bingo. They'd sold a lot of tickets.

Liam took long strides as he made his way to the center. He glanced at the time on his phone. He was eleven minutes late. He moved faster.

When he stepped inside, he was once again confronted with holiday decorations. It was obvious that Christmas wasn't far off. There were white twinkle lights draped back and forth across the ceiling. And in the air was the aroma of buttery popcorn.

On the long lines of tables, there were battery-operated lanterns encircled with green wreaths. And in the front of the room, Mel was sitting at the head table. Next to her stood a six-foot Christmas tree all decorated with a glowing star at the top, and beneath it were a multitude of wrapped packages.

Mel took a small card from Sara Chen and called out, "I—snowman."

The people at the tables rushed to mark their bingo cards.

Sara pulled another card from a basket that had been decorated for the holidays. She once again handed the card to Mel. "G—Santa."

His gaze continued the rest of the way around the room. To his amazement, less than half of the tables were filled. How could that be? The town had been abuzz with excitement over having a new event on the holiday calendar. So where were the other people?

Not wanting to interrupt the game, he lingered in the back. He watched Mel as she called out the cards. She would smile, but her eyes didn't light up, and her face didn't glow. What was going on?

A few minutes later, someone called out, "Bingo." He moved toward the front. He had no idea what to say to Mel, who once again had a forced smile plastered on her face. In the depths of her big brown eyes, he saw something else. Was it worry? Or disappointment? He couldn't be sure. Whatever it was, it wasn't good.

Her father stood off to the side. When Harvey spotted Liam, he said, "I'm glad to see you. I was starting to think you weren't going to show up like the rest of them."

"Where are the others?"

"From what I gather, they're protesting because they think Melinda went over to the dark side by working with Blackwell."

"Are you serious?"

He nodded. "How did you miss all of the drama?"

"I've been working, and I don't hear anything when I'm at the Blackwell mansion." His gaze moved to Mel. "She must be devastated."

"She's putting on a brave face, but I know this is devastating for her."

The bingo winner was directed to a Christmas tree next to Mel that was surrounded by presents. All of the items had been donated to the cause. Liam knew what was in each of them because while Tate had played with his toys, Liam had helped Mel wrap each of them.

She'd really put her heart into this event. It was sad it hadn't turned out the way she'd imagined. What was wrong with people? How could they think she had a bad bone in her body?

Frustrated and feeling helpless, Liam said, "But there has to be something we can do."

Harvey shrugged. "She says to leave it alone. That it'll work itself out."

"Do you agree with her? I mean I've never seen the town act like this. Do they really think Mel would side with Blackwell over them?"

Harvey let out a deep sigh. "I think this is my fault."

Liam turned to Harvey and saw the worry lines etched on his face. He had to say something to bolster the man, who looked like he was carrying the weight of the world on his shoulders. "It'll work out. I'm sure of it. If I know one thing, it's that Bluestar pulls together." His gaze strayed to the empty seats. "It just might take a moment for them to remember that."

"I hope you're right."

There was a slight break before the next round, so Liam made his way to Mel. "Hey. How are you doing?"

"Okay. Are you ready to play?"

He noticed how she skirted around the subject of the lackluster crowd. "I thought I could help you. What do you need me to do?"

Her gaze moved to the half-empty room. "You could play a round or two."

He sent her a tentative smile. "I'd be happy to."

He really didn't want to play bingo, especially now that he knew there was trouble afoot in Bluestar, but it was a simple request, and so he took a seat. And he was finding there wasn't much of anything he wouldn't do for Mel.

—— *ele* ——

Tonight was an utter failure.

What had she been thinking to agree to a deal with Blackwell?

Melinda knew what she'd been thinking about—her father and all of the people on the island that could use better medical care close at hand. Was that such a bad thing? She didn't think so.

She thought for sure her explanation at the Lighthouse Café would have cleared things up with the locals, but it hadn't. There had been a few customers at the bookshop that afternoon, but no more than could be counted on one hand. Business was never this slow during the leadup to Christmas.

Now, she sat at a table on the platform in the Bluestar Hall. She stared out at a mass of empty chairs. There should be people in them. She'd sold enough tickets to fill all of those seats and then some.

She focused on the little card that Sara handed her. "N—snowflake."

"Bingo!" Birdie's face lit up as she held up her bingo card.

Melinda hoped it was indeed a winner, first, because Birdie was the sweetest woman in Bluestar and secondly, because it had been a rough day, and Melinda couldn't wait to go home and drown her sorrows in some ice cream and Christmas cookies from the Elegant Bakery.

Birdie brought her card to Melinda. She quickly verified that she had won. Birdie got the last package under the tree. Sara handed it to her.

Melinda glanced at the package but couldn't remember what was in it. She'd wrapped so many that it was hard to keep track of what was in each package. Everyone was so excited to receive a gift that they'd opened their package while on the stage.

When Birdie didn't make any motion to open the package, Melinda asked, "Aren't you going to open it?"

Birdie nodded. "Oh yes. On Christmas morning."

Melinda nodded. Leave it to Birdie to have more patience than anyone else in the room. Melinda wished she had some of Birdie's patience because she was frustrated with the people she referred to as friends and neighbors. Maybe pushing to build this hospital was a mistake. Maybe she should just let the idea go like the new town council seemed to want to do.

"Oh dear, don't look so glum," Birdie said. "It was a wonderful evening. I haven't had this much fun in a long time. And I even won something. I don't normally win anything. Thank you for planning this evening. It was a lot of fun."

Melinda forced a smile to her lips. "I'm glad you enjoyed it."

"You just wish that others had enjoyed it too."

It was pointless to deny it. Melinda nodded. "I tried to explain it to everyone. I thought they were listening."

"Sometimes it just takes others more time to absorb the information. Hang in there."

"Maybe I shouldn't have made the deal with Blackwell. I never thought it would have this sort of repercussion."

Birdie waved away her words. "If you got that old curmudgeon to agree to spend his money on a good cause, more power to you. Don't let some naysayers stop you. Just keep doing what you're doing. They'll all thank you in the end."

Melinda's gaze searched hers. "Do you really mean that?"

Birdie reached out and patted her arm. "I do. You've got this."

And then Birdie made her way off the platform with the present under her arm. It meant a lot that Birdie believed in the project, but Melinda couldn't help but wonder if Birdie had said all of that just to make her feel better.

"Hey, Melinda," Sara said, "I'm going to start taking down the decorations."

"I can help her," Harvey said.

"Thanks, Dad."

"And I'll help you with the lanterns," Liam said.

"The boxes are behind the stage," Melinda said.

With Liam holding one of the large boxes, she moved to the first table, where she picked up a lantern and turned it off. She popped out the batteries and placed the lantern in the box to be put back in storage with the town's other Christmas decorations.

As they slowly made their way along the long line of tables, his gaze searched hers. "So I've heard a few things, but I wanted to ask you what exactly is going on?"

She glanced around and found her father and Sara working at the other end of the large room. The distance gave her and Liam a little bit of privacy to talk. The last thing she wanted to do was discuss the whole sordid affair...again. But this was Liam, and she knew she could talk to him about anything. She'd learned that when her father was in the hospital. Liam was a great listener.

So she told him about the very quiet day at the bookshop as well as her talk at the Lighthouse Café. "I just can't believe some people would think I would side with Blackwell against them. I would never...ever...do something like that."

"I know that. And so do they."

She paused and stared at him. "Then why have they turned on me?"

Sympathy shone in his eyes. "I think maybe you just surprised them. They didn't see this coming, and it's just going to take them a minute to absorb it all."

He wasn't the first one to tell her that, and she desperately wanted to believe him. Being shunned by so many people was painful and something she'd never felt before. "I just want to fix things."

"And how can you do that?"

Leave it to Liam to make her figure out her own answers. While most people would tell her what they wanted her to do, Liam would just be there with a listening ear, a sturdy shoulder to lean on, and the patience to let her figure out her own problems—like when she told him the bookshop business had slowed down. He hadn't told her what to do. He'd listened and asked questions until she figured out that if she catered to the young readers, then it would bring in the older readers and expand her business.

Maybe this time she'd strived too high. Maybe she had to accept that now wasn't the right time to build the hospital. The acceptance of that statement tugged at her heartstrings. It would mean people like her father wouldn't have immediate access to diagnostic testing and specialized medicine here on the island.

Maybe the right time would be when it wasn't just her pushing so hard for the hospital, but when it was the entire community pushing for it.

There was power in numbers. Being solo was not going to get this done.

"I see the wheels in your mind spinning. What are you thinking?" Liam's voice drew her from her thoughts.

"That I've gone about this all wrong. I need to undo it."

"What does that mean?"

"That I need to speak with Blackwell. What time is it?"

He withdrew his phone from his back pocket. "It's after nine."

She sighed. "It's too late now. I'll have to go first thing in the morning."

"Does this mean you're going to end your arrangement with him?" His tone was neutral, not letting her know if he liked the idea or not.

"Yes. This project is too big for me alone. I need the community to back me."

He was quiet for a moment, as though taking in what she'd told him. "And how do you feel about this?"

She shrugged and then picked up the next lantern. "I'm obviously disappointed and worried about my father's future health care because he hates having to go to the mainland and deal with the hustle and bustle. But I hope this will mend the rift with the community."

But would it? She wouldn't know until she tried. After she spoke with Blackwell in the morning, she'd make sure to "bump" into Agnes Dewey and tell her the news. Agnes was one of the people missing from tonight's bingo. If anyone could get the word out, it would be her.

CHAPTER FIFTEEN

6 days until Christmas...

COME THE MORNING SUN, it was time to act.

Melinda wasn't sure it was the wisest decision, but it was the way things needed to be. She would call off the deal with Blackwell. It wouldn't be the end of her dream of a small hospital on the island, but rather a moment to readjust.

Before heading to the bookshop, she swung by the Blackwell mansion. She knew Blackwell would be up because Liam was already working, and his work was far from quiet.

When she knocked on the door, she was surprised when Liam answered the door. He didn't immediately speak. Instead, his gaze took in her appearance. She wondered if he could tell she hadn't gotten much sleep, but hopefully this would fix her insomnia.

"Hey." His voice was soft. It was like a gentle caress, and she longed to lean into him and feel his strong arms around her, but she refused to let herself give into that desire. "Are you sure you want to do this?"

Not sure she trusted her voice, she nodded.

Liam opened the door wider. "Come in. Mr. Blackwell is in his office."

Melinda stepped inside the home. She couldn't help but glance around. The last time she'd been here, she'd been too nervous to notice much. This time she slowed down and looked around. Everything was covered in dust. She raised her chin and spotted cobwebs on the large chandelier that hung in the middle of the foyer.

She didn't understand it. How could one man be so cheap that he'd rather live in a filthy house than pay for a housekeeper? And no one could convince her that he wasn't rolling in money. He was undoubtedly the richest person on Bluestar Island. And yet he lived like this.

She was beginning to think he wouldn't have had the storm damage repaired if it wasn't for the insurance company picking up the bill. She glanced over to where Liam was working on the grand staircase. She inhaled the scent of fresh wood. She loved the smell.

The steps still needed to be stained, but it was the banister and balusters that drew her attention. Their curves and lines were elegant and sophisticated. It was all too nice for this mess of a house.

When Liam turned back to her and raised a questioning brow, it spurred her into action. She moved toward the office. Blackwell was sitting there, writing in what appeared to be a ledger. There wasn't any sign of a computer in the room.

It took a moment for him to glance up. When he spoke, his tone was harsh. "What do you want?"

Melinda inwardly cringed at his frostiness, but she refused to let him see that it bothered her. No one was going to bully her around. Besides, she was pretty certain his bark was worse than his bite. At least that was what she hoped because she was about to find out if it was true.

She straightened her shoulders and lifted her chin ever so slightly. "I need to talk to you about our agreement."

His gaze lifted over the top of his reading glasses. "Do you have my money for me?"

She reached into her purse and pulled out an envelope. She stepped forward and placed it on his desk. "Here's everything I've collected."

He snatched up the envelope and ripped it open. He counted the money. "This isn't even a quarter of it. Where's the rest?"

She swallowed hard. "That's the thing. I made a mistake by agreeing to do this. I would like to back out of our agreement."

He leaned back in his chair. As he did so the chair creaked, as though it had never been lubricated in its lifetime. The grating sound didn't seem to bother Blackwell in the least.

A wicked smile pulled at his lips as his eyes lit up with delight. "I knew you'd fail. I just had no idea it'd be so easy."

She wasn't surprised he had an agenda, but his boldness floored her. "You mean you expected me to fail?"

"Of course. Why else would I make such a ridiculous deal? There's absolutely no way I'm throwing my money away on some hospital. If people need care, they can go to the mainland."

"Fine. Have it your way, but I think you're making a big mistake by not donating to the new hospital."

"That is what's wrong with you young people. You waste your money instead of saving it."

She imagined him sitting at his desk counting his thousand pieces of gold. But what he didn't seem to understand was that no amount of money could bring him happiness. And from what she saw, he wasn't very happy.

"Money is nice, but it can't keep you company." As he frowned at her, she continued. "It can't comfort you. And in the end, you can't take it with you."

"Not true. You can be buried with it. I checked."

She rolled her eyes. Why was she not surprised he'd asked a mortician if he could take his money with him?

"You do realize that instead of counting your money, you could make other people around you happy with it."

He frowned at her. "Why would I want to do that? No one bothers with me. Why would I bother with them?"

"Maybe if you give the people of Bluestar a chance, you would be surprised by their kindness."

"Bwaa..." He shook his head. "So you're admitting that you failed?"

"No. I want to call if off." When he continued to blankly stare at her, she said, "You know, forget that we ever made the deal."

He shook his head. "It's not going to happen. A deal is a deal. And now I'm going to take possession of the bookshop in the New Year."

Her heart clenched at the thought of losing the bookshop. "What if I fight you?"

He opened a desk drawer and pulled out their signed agreement. "I'll show the judge this agreement with your signature."

"I could claim that I was tricked."

He leaned forward, resting his arms on the edge of the desk. "Tsk. Tsk. Would you really lie? I didn't think you would do such a thing."

She inwardly groaned. Why was this man so infuriating? It would be so easy to lower herself to his level, but that would mean she was no better than him. And she just couldn't lower herself that far. Even if it meant she had to close her bookshop.

The thought caused the backs of her eyes to sting with unshed tears. She blinked repeatedly. She refused to let Blackwell see how much he was hurting her.

"I won't lie."

"Good. I have plans for that building. It'll make me a lot of money."

"You can't do that!" Liam's voice came from behind her.

She turned to find Liam standing in the open doorway. His hands were resting on his trim waist.

His brows were drawn together as his gaze zeroed in on Blackwell. She'd never seen Liam look so formidable.

Blackwell got to his feet. "I can! And I will! You aren't going to stop me."

"Yes, I will." Liam strode toward the man.

Liam was north of six feet with broad shoulders. On the other hand, Blackwell was maybe five-six and not muscular at all. There was definitely no contest between them.

Melinda stepped in his way. "Liam, stop. This is my fight not yours."

"He can't just go around destroying people with absolutely no repercussion." Liam glared at Blackwell. "You can't close the Seaside Bookshop."

"I can. And I will. You know what else I can do?"

Liam pressed his lips into a firm line and glared at the man. Melinda willed Liam to remain quiet. Things were spiraling out of control. And she knew no matter what Liam said that Blackwell wouldn't change his mind about the bookshop. He'd been pushing for her to move out since he bought the building. At last he had his chance to get the storefront, and there was no way he'd back down.

"Mr. Blackwell..." Melinda tried to gain the man's attention, but the two men were glaring at each other.

"You're fired. Get..." Blackwell reached for the desk with his left hand. He lowered his head, letting his gaze move to the desktop. "G... G..."

Her mind raced to figure out what was going on. Something wasn't right. She wasn't sure what was going on. "Mr. Blackwell, are you okay?"

He dropped down into his chair. When he raised his head, it looked as though the right side of his face was sagging.

"G..." He attempted to speak, but all that would come out were just unintelligible sounds.

She glanced over at Liam. Immediately, his stance changed. He moved toward Blackwell. He knelt down next to him. "Mr. Blackwell, can you say your name?"

"W... Uh..." The man's face contorted into a look of frustration.

"Can you lift your left arm?"

At first, Blackwell just sat there, as though he wasn't sure what he was supposed to do. Liam tapped his arm. "Lift it."

Blackwell lifted his arm.

Liam patted his right arm. "Lift this arm."

Blackwell didn't move.

Liam patted the same arm again. "Can you move this arm?"

Blackwell groaned but nothing happened.

Melinda was swept back in time to the past summer when her father had a heart attack. The anxiety and worry swept over her. This wasn't the same situation, and yet she felt a similar rush of emotions.

She'd come so close to losing her father that day. She'd never been more afraid in her life. She knew Blackwell wasn't her father, but it didn't stop the rush of panic.

She hadn't been there when her father had his medical emergency, and she always felt so guilty. She didn't know what she could have done to help her father, but she was here now. She could do something to help Mr. Blackwell.

Liam turned to her. "Call 911. Tell them we have a possible stroke. We're going to need to transport him to the mainland asap."

Melinda's heart raced as she dialed her phone and relayed Liam's instructions. They said the ambulance would be there in a few minutes, and that life flight had been alerted. The only question was how long would it take for the chopper to reach the island.

Hurry. Please hurry.

She didn't know much about strokes, but she'd heard if they were treated quickly, it was less likely the patient would have lasting effects. She hoped that would be the case.

Blackwell continued to try to speak. Nothing but slurs and groans came out. His eyes were wide with fear.

Sympathy oozed from her. She went to Blackwell's side and knelt down next to him. It had to be a good sign that he was still conscious and making attempts to speak.

She instinctively took his hand in hers. "You're going to be okay. Help is on the way."

He gripped her hand tightly. He attempted to speak, but she couldn't make out anything he uttered. It was the first time she saw true fear in his eyes.

She didn't know how long she knelt by his side, doing her best to reassure him that he would be all right. Every time he stared into her eyes with that wide-eyed panic, her heart would clench.

Even though it was only a matter of minutes, it felt like an eternity until the paramedics showed up. As they helped Blackwell onto a gurney, he clung to her hand. She promised him that she'd meet him at the hospital.

After they'd taken Blackwell away, Liam asked, "Why did you tell him that?"

She looked at him in total confusion. "What? You mean about seeing him at the hospital?" When Liam nodded, she said, "Because the man doesn't have any family here on the island. To be honest, I don't know if he has any family anywhere."

Softly Liam said, "Mel, he's not your father."

His words poked at a tender spot in her chest. "I know that." The words came out harsher than she'd meant. "I'm sorry. I'm just worried."

"I know. It's never easy to see someone suffering."

Her gaze searched his. "But you used to be a paramedic. It's got to be easier for you."

He shrugged. "I've learned to compartmentalize my feelings. I might not show it, but some calls get to me. I just have to push all of that aside and do what needs to be done."

She nodded in understanding. "I just want to make this easier for him."

Liam's gaze searched hers. "But he was so mean to you. He's taking away your bookshop."

She lowered her gaze. "I know. And I hate that he's doing that, but then I look at him and he looks so small and needy. He's a lonely old man who is scared and has no one to reach out to."

It would be so easy to hate the man, but she fought the urge. She couldn't help but hope this incident would change the man. But that wasn't the reason she was going to the hospital. It was simply the compassionate thing to do.

It'd been more than three hours.

And yet it felt like an eternity.

Melinda paced the black-and-white-tiled floor of the waiting area of a mainland emergency room while Liam sat in one of the plastic chairs. She had yet to see Blackwell. When she'd asked to see him, to make sure he was all right, she'd been told he had been taken for testing. They would let her know when she could go back and visit with him.

As more people moved into the waiting area, she decided to sit down. No need to annoy them with her pacing.

"He looked so scared," she whispered to Liam.

"He's lucky you were there."

"But you were there too."

"I was working. Quite honestly, I hardly interact with him during the day. I might not have known anything was wrong."

Blackwell didn't make it easy for anyone to care about him. She didn't understand how someone would close themselves off. She loved to interact with the residents of Bluestar Island as well as the tourists that visited in the summer.

"Do you think he'll be okay?" Her gaze searched Liam's, needing some sign of hope.

"I don't know."

Her pent-up anxiety and the memory of Blackwell staring into her eyes with such desperation and fear as he clung to her hand had her own emotions strung high. "How can you not know? You're a paramedic. You must have experience with these sorts of situations."

He was quiet for a moment, as though carefully choosing his words. "Every case is different."

"Can't you just say if this is life threatening or if you think he'll be okay?" Her gaze pleaded with him to give her words of encouragement—something she could cling to.

She remembered too well sitting in this very emergency room and waiting on word about her father. It was only six months ago, and the wounds were still fresh. That day she'd come ever so close to losing her own father, and that could never happen again. It was the reason she'd worked so hard to fund a hospital on Bluestar Island.

"Just relax." Liam reached out, covering her hand with his own. He gave it a squeeze.

She found comfort in his touch. Before she could turn over her hand and clasp his hand, he pulled away. Immediately, she missed his touch.

"I'm so sorry I got you fired. I never meant for that to happen."

"It wasn't your fault." His gaze didn't meet hers.

The door to the emergency room opened, and a nurse stepped out. She glanced around the room and then started in their direction. Melinda's heart beat faster in anticipation. Was there at last some news?

"Ms. Coleman, you can come back now."

She stood to follow the nurse but then turned back to Liam. "Are you coming?"

He shook his head. "You've got this."

She didn't have time to argue with him as the nurse kept going. Melinda rushed to catch up to her. After they passed through the locked door, she was led through a maze of hallways with curtained cubicles.

At last, the nurse stopped and gestured to a bed. "He's in here. He listed you on his paperwork as his emergency contact."

"He did?" She didn't know what to make of that information.

The nurse nodded as she lifted a digital notebook. "If I could just have your phone number."

"But doesn't he have some family he'd rather have do it?"

"Apparently not." The nurse frowned. "Would you rather not be listed?"

"No, erm... I mean it's okay." Melinda gave her phone number, and the nurse noted it in her file. "Does this mean I can call to check on him?"

The nurse nodded. "You can go in now."

"Thank you." Melinda's body tensed because she wasn't sure what to expect—the scared man that had clung to her hand or the mean and nasty man who only cared about his money and not the people's lives he was about to ruin in his ruthless pursuit of more wealth.

Melinda drew in a deep breath and slowly blew it out. She straightened her shoulders and then she walked to his bedside. His eyes were closed, and he looked so small in that bed covered with white blankets. His white hair was messed up, and his glasses were off. He didn't look like the same man who had threatened to take away her beloved bookshop.

She worried her bottom lip as her gaze lowered to her hands. She wasn't sure if she should say something or just let him rest.

"You...are still here." His voice was a bit raspy, but she could make out the words.

Her gaze rose to meet his. She smiled at him. "How are you doing?"

"Better." There was an awkward pause. "Thank you."

Melinda couldn't help but wonder if she'd imagined those words. She'd never once in her life heard him utter those two words, but then again she never spent much time with him. Maybe at last he was changing. "You're welcome. I'm just glad I was there to help you."

"This doesn't change anything. A deal is a deal."

The spark of hope was quickly snuffed out. "Is there anything I can do for you?"

"My house. Can you take care of it?"

"Um...sure."

"There's a key...under the flower pot."

"Okay. Don't worry. Your house will be fine."

"Someone might break-in."

She shook her head. "It's Bluestar. That's never going to happen."

His eyes filled with worry. "Just keep an eye on it 'til I get there."

"I will. I promise."

Melinda stayed a few more minutes, but she quickly ran out of things to talk to him about. He wasn't exactly a chatty person. She supposed that was to be expected since he was basically a hermit.

After seeing him, she felt more confident about him returning to the island. And now she needed to get back to the island because for the moment, she still had a bookshop to run.

CHAPTER SIXTEEN

W HAT SHOULD HE SAY?

Liam noticed how quiet Mel had been on the way back to the island. He didn't know if she was worried about Blackwell, losing her bookshop, or both. And he didn't know what to say to comfort her.

On the ferry ride back to the island, he talked about random, irrelevant things. He talked about the weather and that they were calling for a white Christmas that year. She didn't say anything. He mentioned that there was a Christmas movie at the community center that evening. He asked her to guess what movie they picked this year. She didn't speak.

He checked the time. It was just after one in the afternoon. "I suppose you need to get to the bookshop."

She shook her head. "I called Ava from the hospital, and she said that there wasn't much business. I told her to close up and go home."

He turned to her. "Don't give up."

She shrugged. "What am I supposed to do? The community is upset with me."

"Not all of them. Just some of them. They'll come around. They'll understand you were just trying to help the community."

Her gaze met his. "I hope you're right. I've never had so many people upset with me."

He reached out, taking her hand into his own. He gave it a squeeze. "Trust me. This is all going to work out."

She shook her head. "I just don't see how."

Neither did he at that moment, but he didn't admit it to her. Maybe he shouldn't have said it. After all, he didn't want Mel to be hurt further. And the only way to keep that from happening was for him to find a way to mend things.

It wouldn't be easy. In fact, it would border on impossible. But with Mel's hand clasped with his, he felt as though he were capable of great things if it meant helping her. His thumb gently massaged the back of her hand. He would find a way to make it better for her.

"So, without the bookshop to run, what will you do with the rest of your day off?"

She shrugged. "I don't know. Maybe check in on my dad."

"Or... You can come back to my place. Tate will be happy to see you."

She shook her head. "Thanks. I don't think so. I'm not good company right now."

"All the more reason to come over. You need a distraction. And if I'm not enough of one, then Tate will have to charm you."

At the mention of his son, a smile came over her face. It was the first time he'd seen her smile all day. "He wouldn't have to work hard. Your son is adorable. You're so lucky to have him."

"I couldn't agree more." As they stepped off the ferry onto Bluestar Island, he said, "Let's go get Tate."

"Lead the way."

Minutes later they picked up Tate from his brother's place. He carried Tate up to his second-floor apartment. He opened the door and stepped aside for Mel to enter first.

"Don't mind the mess. Tate was up early this morning, and I didn't get a chance to pick up his toys."

"It's fine." She slipped off her coat and looked around. "You don't have a Christmas tree."

He shrugged. "I didn't get to it."

"But you have to have a Christmas tree, right, Tate?"

"Yeah!" His son grinned up at him.

Liam was pretty certain his son had no idea what he was agreeing to. He just liked to see Mel smile—just like his dad.

He put Tate down. Before his son could run off, he took off his snow boots and then unzipped his coat. Liam pulled off his son's mittens and helped him out of his coat.

Tate ran off to the bedroom and quickly returned with a truck in his hand. He showed it to Mel. "Monster truck," he said in a deep voice before, dropping down to his knees and pushing the truck over the floor. "Vroom!"

"Can I play too?" Mel asked.

Tate paused. He nodded his head as he reached for one of his plastic trucks on the floor. He picked up a green and white one and held it out to her. "It's a garbage truck."

She took it from him. "Thank you."

Liam stood off to the side and watched as Tate and Mel played with their trucks. Mel's face lit up with a smile that went the whole way to her eyes. Liam couldn't imagine his life without Tate... Or Mel. Day by day the three of them were getting closer—almost like a family. He refused to let himself dwell on the thought.

While Mel and Tate played, Liam moved about the small apartment, straightening things up. He rinsed off some dishes and placed them in the dishwasher to run later.

Once he completed his tasks, he turned to find Mel seated on the floor with her back against the couch. Tate had moved on to playing with his building blocks. Mel quietly sat there, watching Tate.

As though she sensed Liam staring at her, her gaze rose to meet his. He couldn't tell what she was thinking, but as their gazes held, his heart beat faster. In that moment, he could imagine this scenario of Mel playing with Tate and him doing household chores becoming a permanent arrangement.

The thought startled him. Ever since his marriage had imploded, he'd told himself he just wasn't cut out to be a husband. So, why had the thought come to his mind?

Having no answer, he glanced away and made a big deal of straightening the hand towel on the countertop. The strangeness of the day was jolting to him. That was it. Nothing more.

And maybe it was the coziness of his apartment. He hadn't thought about that when he'd invited her over. They needed to do something—anything to get them out of the place so he could breathe some fresh air. It would help clear his mind.

"What would you like to do now?" His gaze returned to hers but only briefly this time before he turned his attention to Tate.

"We could go get a Christmas tree."

Liam inwardly groaned. She would pick that. Decorating a Christmas tree was what families did together. They weren't a family, even if it was easy to imagine.

But what was the alternative? To stay here and stare deeply into her eyes. His heart beat faster at the thought. If anything, he'd rather go buy some mistletoe, and then they could pick up that kiss where they'd left off.

Whoa! He pulled his rambling thoughts up short. It was definitely time for a distraction. "Let's go get a Christmas tree."

The day had started awfully.

But Liam and Tate had made it much better.

They strolled in the softly falling snow to the tree lot in the center of town. Tate picked out the tallest tree on the lot. It was far too tall for their apartment. Then Liam picked out a fir tree, but Melinda pointed out that it had a crooked trunk. She picked out a blue spruce that was as tall as her, so she knew it would fit in the apartment, and it wouldn't be too hard for them to carry home. Liam and Tate agreed on the tree.

It was on the way back to Liam's place that they ran into Birdie. Instead of walking, she was riding in her golf cart. Melinda was relieved to see the woman was using caution especially after her fall last year that ended up landing her in the hospital and then physical rehab.

They told her about Blackwell and how his prognosis was quite good in spite of the delay in transporting him to the mainland. They also told her about the Seaside Bookshop closing and how Liam had lost his job. Birdie told them how sorry she was for them, but not to give up. This was the time of the year when the most unexpected things happened.

Melinda ran back to her place to pick up some decorations to loan to Liam. When she returned, the little Christmas tree was anchored in a tree stand in the corner of Liam's apartment, and Mel smiled.

Once the twinkle lights were strung, Melinda was assigned the task of attaching the hooks to the ornaments. Liam helped Tate hang them on the tree. But Tate was easily distracted, so Liam took over hanging the ornaments.

With only a few ornaments left, she took them and moved toward the tree. They were smaller glass balls. She placed them near the top of the tree.

"There," she said. "What do you think?"

He stepped back. "I think it looks good."

She joined him and stared at the tree. "There's something missing." She moved to the box of decorations she'd brought from her place. She rummaged around until she found what she wanted. She lifted an angel. She fluffed the angel's white dress and straightened the wings.

She held it out for him to see. "What do you think?"

He shrugged. "It looks like an angel."

She smiled and shook her head. "No. I mean do you want it on top of the tree?"

"Sure." When she held it out to him, he shook his head. "You go ahead and put it on."

She moved to the tree and reached up, but she was too short to situate the angel atop the tree. "I can't reach."

Liam grabbed a wooden chair from the table and moved it next to the tree. "Try this."

He held his hand out to her. She placed her hand in his. Immediately, there was a shiver of awareness that tingled her fingers. The sensation worked its way up her arm and settled in her chest. Her heart beat faster, and her breath came quickly.

Her gaze lowered to his mouth. If only she'd put some mistletoe in the box of decorations. She stifled a sigh. She raised her gaze to meet his. A little smile pulled at the corner of his lips. She'd been caught staring at him.

The moment seemed to halt as she waited and wondered if he was going to kiss her. Did she want him too? Oh yes. Was it the smart thing to do? Probably not.

She stared into his eyes, unable to turn away. There was an emotion reflected in his eyes, but she couldn't name it. Or perhaps she was afraid to figure it out. Because she was in absolutely no position to start anything with anyone—most especially her best friend. Her life as she knew it was slowly and agonizingly imploding.

And yet when she was here with Liam and Tate, she felt as though she were wrapped in a warm quilt of happiness. It was as though the rest of her problems were locked out in the cold and snow—unable to reach her when she was here with them.

Liam glanced away. And in a blink of an eye, the moment passed. She gave herself a mental shake as she stepped up onto the chair and placed the angel atop the tree. It took a little bit of maneuvering as she plugged in the lights. The little candle lights in the angel's hands lit up.

Melinda leaned back. Not too bad. She stepped down. "What do you think?"

"I don't know. Let's see." He moved to the light switch near the doorway and flicked off the lights.

The room was bathed in the soft glow from the Christmas tree. Liam stepped up next to her and in that moment, she forgot about the tree with its colorful twinkle lights and how hard she'd worked to make it special for him and Tate. In that moment, she was only aware of the man standing next to her.

Her pulse raced. She didn't dare turn to him. She didn't want him to see the rush of conflicting emotions in her eyes. She didn't want to ruin their friendship. Things were already so complicated between them after she'd cost him his job with Blackwell.

As though he could read her thoughts, he reached out, taking her hand in his warm grasp. His fingers laced with hers. Nothing had ever felt so right.

In a peaceful silence, they stood there, staring at the Christmas tree with its twinkling lights and glittering ornaments. It was beautiful—not just the tree but this whole evening. In spite of everything that had gone down with Blackwell, Liam had created this magical evening. It was like a balm on her bruised heart.

At last, she worked up the courage to turn to him. She didn't let go of his hand. It was as though she were channeling strength from their connection.

She gazed up at him. "Thank you."

"I'm the one that should be thanking you. The tree looks fantastic."

She shook her head. "I mean thank you for taking a perfectly awful day and turning it into something magical. I'll never forget this evening."

And then he did something totally unexpected. He released her hand, and in the next heartbeat, he pulled her into his arms. Her head came to rest on his shoulder. She could hear his heart beat. It was beating fast, just like her own.

She felt as though they were two puzzle pieces that fit together. If it was possible to make this moment go on forever, she would do it. In his arms, she felt that anything was possible.

But she knew it wasn't reality. She couldn't hide from her problems—not even in Liam's arms. With the greatest of regret, she pulled away.

"And thank you for bringing Christmas to our house. I know Tate will love it when he wakes up." He glanced over at his son, who curled up in the arm chair and rubbed his eyes as he yawned.

"It was nothing."

He arched a disbelieving brow. "So you're saying you loan out your holiday decorations to just anyone?"

"No. Definitely not." Her collection of ornaments spanned back to her grandmother. They were a collection of memories filled with love. "I just meant that I enjoyed it too. It was what I needed to take my mind off my problems." And as much as she wanted to stay, she knew things had become much too cozy. Unless she wanted to complicate her life even more, she should leave. "And now I should go."

"But what about the Christmas movie?" He looked expectantly at her.

It was a new item on Bluestar's Christmas calendar. They were having a pajama party and playing a movie at the community center. Aster Bell, Bluestar's events coordinator, had been very busy organizing events to draw the community together.

Melinda's gaze moved to Tate as he fell asleep on the chair. "I don't think you should wake him."

"I agree. That's why I was thinking we could stay here and watch a movie. I'll even toss in a pizza and pop us some popcorn."

She stared at him for a moment, just to make sure he was serious. "I can't believe you want to spend more time with me. We've been together all day."

"And I've been looking forward to watching a Christmas movie all day. So, what do you say?"

Somehow she didn't think watching a holiday movie was high on his list, but there was no place she wanted to be. And if she went home right now, she wouldn't do anything but worry...about costing Liam his job...about losing the chance for a new hospital...about losing the bookshop. The thoughts tugged on her heartstrings.

Liam stepped in front of her. With a finger beneath her chin, he lifted her head until their gazes met. "Stop worrying. Everything is going to work out."

"How can you say that?" She didn't think anything was going to be all right ever again.

He lowered his hand, but their gazes continued to connect. "Because it's the season for some Christmas magic."

She felt as though her holiday sparkle had fizzled and burned out. "You're just saying that to make me feel better."

"Yes, I am. But I also believe it. You just have to stay positive. Where there's a will, there's a way."

She wanted to believe him. "Then I should go work on finding the way."

He shook his head. "You've had a big day. Problem-solving requires some rest and some nutrients."

She was impressed with how hard he was working for her to stay. And frankly she didn't have the will or the energy to fight him. The couch looked inviting, and her stomach rumbled its hunger.

"Only if you agree to get extra pepperoni."

"Of course. Is there any other way to order a pizza?"

She smiled at him. He smiled back, making her heart flutter. She sat on the couch and reached for the remote. "Do you have a particular movie in mind?"

"No. Whatever you pick will be fine."

"You might be sorry you said that." And then she set to work searching through the on-demand movies. There were so many to pick from.

The day had started miserably, but it was ending on a much better note, thanks to Liam. What would she ever do without him? She hoped she'd never find out. But without her bookshop, she didn't know if her future would be here on the island.

CHAPTER SEVENTEEN

5 days before Christmas...

TODAY'S HOLIDAY ACTIVITY WAS the Christmas cookie and gingerbread house contest. And somehow Liam had been roped into being a judge. It happened when Mel and Birdie had ganged up on him. All he could remember was saying no, but somewhere along the way his answer turned into a yes. When those two put their minds together, there wasn't anything they couldn't accomplish.

But having to meet up at the community center for the contest and knowing a lot of the townsfolk would be in attendance gave him an idea. And so, with Tate bathed and dressed in some of his nicer clothes, i.e. ones without any stains, they'd headed out early. This event might present a chance to fix things for Mel. At least he hoped so. When he arrived at the hall and learned Mel was running a few minutes behind, he decided to seize the opportunity. Leaving Tate with Sara Chen, he climbed up onto the stage. A hush fell over the crowd.

He cleared his throat. "I just need a moment of your time."

"When is the contest going to start?" Agnes Dewey asked. "My white chocolate macadamia nut cookies are a shoo-in."

"Soon. I promise. I just need a moment to speak to you all." He stared out at the sea of confused expressions. "I know some of you are still upset with Mel...Melinda for making a deal with Blackwell, but I want you to know that she only did it with the best of intentions. She wanted desperately to come up with the remaining money for the hospital. And I think we all know that Blackwell could bank roll that hospital."

"That's because he's a cranky cheapskate!" a male voice called out from the back of the room.

"She shouldn't have agreed to do his dirty work!"

"It wasn't right. She was our friend."

Liam nodded. "I understand. I was shocked when I heard the news, but I knew she'd done it out of the goodness of her heart." He glanced at Joe Saunders. "You know how caring she can be. Didn't she mow your grass this summer when your arthritis was acting up?"

The older man bobbed his bald head. "Yeah. She did. And she refused to let me pay her."

"And, Betty, didn't she organize a food chain when your family was down with the flu?"

Betty nodded. "She did."

"And she organized all of the activities at the bookshop."

"And she worked so hard to raise money for the hospital."

"That's right," Liam said. "She did all of that. And that's why you should give her a break."

A murmur cascaded through the crowd. Surely they had to get over their hurt feelings and realize they'd always cared about Mel. She was still the same person.

"You should also know that yesterday morning, she went to Blackwell's house to back out of the deal, but he is insisting on sticking to the agreement."

"It sounds like him. He's always looking out for himself."

Liam decided to ignore the comment because quite honestly, he couldn't argue with them. "Mel is now in danger of losing the bookshop if she doesn't come up with all of the rent money."

"So she's still in cahoots with Blackwell."

Liam shook his head. "No. She isn't. She told him she was done."

"But what about her bookshop?"

"There's a good possibility she's going to lose it. Unless we do something to stop that from happening." He dodged the ensuing questions as he stepped off the stage.

He knew not to push too hard. People needed time to digest the information. He just had to hope they came to the right conclusion—they couldn't let Mel lose the bookshop.

In the end, it didn't take people nearly as long to do the right thing as he'd imagined. Because people approached him. Some gave him a check for their rent and others didn't have money on them but insisted they'd get the money to him shortly.

Liam was reassured by this outpouring. Now he just had to hope they would be as warm and compassionate to Mel.

———*ele*———

She was late.

She hated being late for anything.

Melinda placed the last Santa Mitten cookie on the tray. The cookie recipe had belonged to her grandmother and was handed down to her mother and now to her. Whereas her grandmother used to frost the cookies, her mother changed it to red and white sprinkles. When Melinda took over the recipe, she changed the white sprinkles on the cuff of the mittens to white chocolate with red sanding sugar.

She rearranged the cookies so they evenly covered the tray. They hadn't turned out too bad. She didn't know if they would win, but at least they looked pretty.

She glanced at the clock. If she didn't leave now she'd be disqualified from the contest. She couldn't let that happen after all of the work she'd done to come up with a dozen perfect cookies. Her gaze strayed to the sink filled with dirty dishes. It couldn't be for nothing.

Ding.

She pulled her phone from her purse. It was a message from Liam.

Are you on your way?

She hesitated. Would she be welcome at the event? Then she realized that by living in a small town, it wasn't like she could hide from people. She was going to run into those same people every day. It was best to just let them get their frustrations off their chests now.

Her fingers moved over the screen of her phone. *On my way.*

She secured the lid on the cookie container, slipped on her snow boots and her coat. She decided to drive her cart. She didn't have time to walk, and she didn't want to take a chance of slipping on ice and messing up her cookies.

When she arrived at the community center, she wasn't sure what to expect. As she went to hang up her coat, Hannah Bell offered to hold her coat for her. They made small talk about the competition as Hannah, being the owner of the Elegant Bakery, had been chosen as one of the judges.

Melinda made her way to the table and placed her cookies next to some Grinch cookies that were elaborately decorated. And on the other side were church cookies with all of the trimmings, including a dash of snow on the roof. There was no way her cookies were going to place against such stiff competition. Oh well, the baking had taken her mind off of other issues, like begging Blackwell not to evict her from the building.

As soon as the troubling thought came to her, she pushed it aside. There was nothing she could do about it with Blackwell still in the hospital. She'd called earlier in the day to check on him and spoke to one of his nurses. To her relief, he had greatly improved. Melinda was happy to hear the news, even if he wasn't a very nice man.

Her thoughts were interrupted as people kept coming up to her. They complimented her cookies and apologized for jumping to the wrong conclusion about her arrangement with Blackwell. She was happy things were finally straightened out, but she didn't understand what had precipitated this sudden change in people's minds.

Agnes Dewey made her way over to her. "Nice cookies, too bad they aren't good enough to beat my gingerbread poinsettia cookies."

Melinda supposed that was Agnes's version of a compliment. "Yours look very nice."

"And they taste delicious. Just wait until the judges get to them." Agnes looked quite pleased with herself.

"Well, good luck."

"Oh luck isn't necessary. This is all about skill. And I've been baking longer than you've been alive."

What in the world was she supposed to say to that? Melinda was left speechless. Agnes was definitely one of the more colorful people in Bluestar.

Agnes continued to stand there instead of moving on. "I heard you tried to get out of your deal with Blackwell."

Melinda swallowed hard. "You did?"

Agnes nodded. "Liam told us all about it. You should have known better than to agree to anything with that man. He's only out for himself."

And then Agnes walked away, leaving Melinda once again speechless. So Liam was going around telling people what had happened. She wasn't sure how she felt about that. She knew he was only trying to watch out for her, but she could take care of herself. He didn't need to worry about her.

She was about to go tell him that when the contest got underway. And since he was one of the judges, she shouldn't speak to him. Instead, she moved to the back of the room, where she got a glass of fruit punch and a sugar cookie.

"I saw your cookies," Birdie said. "They looked very nice."

"Thanks. But I don't think they'll stand up to the other ones up there."

"You never know. It isn't all about looks. It's what's on the inside that counts."

Were they still talking about cookies? Melinda wasn't so sure. Her gaze moved to the other end of the room where she saw Liam take a bite of a holly-leaf-shaped cookie. He made some notations on his clipboard.

"He's a really good guy." Birdie nodded toward Liam.

"He is. I'm lucky to have a friend like him."

"Yes, you are, but you have other people that care about you too. No one wants to see you lose the bookshop, and that's why people have been giving Liam their rent money."

"But I backed out of that deal."

"Blackwell would never stand for that. And so, we all want to do our part to keep you in business." Birdie met her gaze. "You can't let him win. Do not give up. Where will we get our books otherwise?"

"I... I don't know." She blinked repeatedly, attempting to keep a rush of emotions at bay.

"Keep your chin up. This is all going to work out." Birdie patted her arm before she moved on.

As Melinda stood there with her glass of punch, more people came up to her. Some gave her their rent checks and others offered their apologies for jumping to the wrong conclusion.

When the evening was over, Melinda's cookies didn't win, but they did come in third place. However, she won in the hearts of her neighbors. Things were getting back to normal. It was one of the best Christmas presents ever. She didn't know until that moment just how much the community of Bluestar meant to her.

CHAPTER EIGHTEEN

4 days until Christmas…

THE BIG DAY WAS almost upon them.

Liam had to hurry. Now that he was no longer working for Blackwell, he had some free time on his hands. After spending the morning building a toy train set with Tate, they had an early lunch. Liam realized that if he was going to finish making some Christmas presents, he needed to get to work.

While Tate played with his toys, Liam set to work, finishing some of the projects in his woodshop. The bookshelf he'd started for Mel was almost complete. A little more sanding and it'd be ready to stain.

He imagined the smile on Mel's face when she saw it. He also had one other small gift for her. He'd finished it already. It was a wooden bookmark with a little Christmas tree etched into the wood. He never wanted her to forget the evening they decorated his tree together.

In the middle of the afternoon, his phone rang. It was Madison St. Claire. He froze as he stared at the caller ID. Was this good news? Or bad? *Please let it be good news.*

He drew in a deep breath and slowly blew it out as he pressed the phone to his ear. "Hello."

"Hey, Liam, am I interrupting anything?"

He glanced at the bookcase. "Nothing that can't wait."

"Good. I was hoping you could meet me this afternoon." She rattled off the address. "I think this house will really suit you and your son."

Hope swelled in his chest. "Is this the house you mentioned before?"

"It is. And they're anxious to sell, so the price is quite reasonable." She named a price that was lower than what she'd originally told him.

He leaned back against the workbench as he absorbed this information. The asking price was low enough that he had enough in his savings for the downpayment without the money that Blackwell owed him. This could really work out.

"Sounds good." He struggled to restrain his excitement. This was still far from a certain thing. "I'll see you there."

After he disconnected the call, he and Tate cleaned up their things. He wanted to swing by the Seaside Bookshop. He was worried about Mel. She didn't complain about the mess she was in with Blackwell, but he could tell it was eating at her.

Between the two of them, they'd collected a number of rent payments. As word spread through Bluestar about the bookshop being on the line, they didn't have to go to the people. Instead, the renters were coming to them with their payments and giving their wishes that the bookshop would remain open.

Liam didn't have a copy of the official list of renters, so he had no idea how many more people owed Blackwell their rent. He wanted to believe that everyone would come through for Mel, but he also understood that Blackwell was not a good landlord; he routinely increased people's rent and failed to make timely repairs.

The more he thought about Blackwell, the tighter his fingers became on the steering wheel of the cart. He wondered if that man had always been so miserable or if it was just something that had come over him later in life. Either way, Blackwell would never have any friends. No one could treat people with such disregard and expect anyone to like them.

They parked near the bookshop and walked along the shoveled sidewalk. All the while Tate chattered on about wanting a truck book. Liam wasn't certain what a truck book was, but he was certain Tate would show him.

As they entered the bookshop, he was relieved to find the place filled with customers, young and old alike. When he spotted Mel behind the checkout counter, she was smiling. It was such a relief.

After he removed Tate's coat, his son ran over to a nearby bookshelf displaying the children's books. Liam smiled and shook his head. His son was a quick learner and knew exactly where to find the books he liked.

After Mel finished with a customer, he stepped up to the counter. He angled his body so he was able to keep an eye on his son. "Hi."

"Hi." She once more smiled, but it didn't go the whole way to her eyes.

"I brought over a couple of more rent payments that people gave me." He withdrew the envelope from his coat pocket and handed it to her. "Do you have it all yet?"

She reached beneath the counter. She lifted a smallish gray metal box. She opened it and withdrew a slip of paper. "It's a good thing I kept a copy of the list of renters and what I'd turned over to Blackwell." She marked off the additional rent payments. "There's only a couple that are outstanding."

Hope swelled in his chest. "That's great. You'll be able to turn over the payments to Blackwell and keep your bookshop."

"I hope so." She glanced around at the bookshop. "I don't know what I was thinking to risk all of this."

"You were doing what you always do—trying to help people."

She placed the payments in the box, closed the lid, and placed it beneath the counter. "What has you out and about?"

"Well, Tate wanted a truck book. And I wanted to give you those checks."

"Thank you. I really appreciate what you did, you know, talking with everyone before the baking competition."

He shrugged off her nice words. "It's nothing you wouldn't have done for me."

"But we both know that's not true. It's my fault you lost your job with Blackwell. I'm so sorry. I will speak to him when he gets out of the hospital."

"How's he doing?" He knew Mel well enough to know she would keep up on Blackwell's progress.

"I don't know all of the details, but since he added me to his medical forms, the hospital told me he had a T-I-A, a mini stroke. And his symptoms have already resolved themselves. I hear he's making a ruckus and threatening to walk out the door if they don't release him."

Liam shook his head. "I'd like to say that I'm surprised, but I'm not."

"Neither am I. I thought for sure he'd need to go to physical rehab for a while, but it doesn't appear that's going to happen because he won't let it." Her gaze met his, causing his heart to pound against his ribs. "Are you and Tate going sled riding later?"

"I think so." He checked the time. It was almost time to meet Madison at the house. "Is there any chance you could slip away for a little bit?"

"I don't know." She glanced around at the customers. "What did you have in mind?"

He glanced around to make sure they weren't overheard, and then he lowered his voice. "We're going to see a house. Want to go with us? I could really use someone else's input."

"That's great!" She pressed her rosy lips together, as though realizing her exclamation had come out too loud. "Sorry. I'm really happy for you."

"So you'll do it? You'll come with us?"

"I'd like to," Mel said. "But I can't just leave Ava here alone."

"Yes, you can." Ava stepped up beside her. "You haven't taken a break all day. Now go." She smiled at them. "I've got this."

In no time, they were headed across town to the craftsman house on a quiet street with a big fenced-in yard. Liam was blown away by how easily he could imagine raising Tate there. If the inside was as good as the outside, he was totally sold.

He glanced at Mel as she took in the place. She was being too quiet. He had to know if she thought it had promise. "What do you think?"

"I really like it. I can't wait to see the inside."

"Me too."

The front door opened, and Madison St. Claire waved to them from the large covered porch, where Liam could imagine kicking back after a long day. There was something special about this place. He easily imagine calling it his home.

They stepped inside. There was a long hallway that led the whole way to the back of the house. On the left side was a great room that included the living room, dining room, and kitchen. To the right were two bedrooms with a bathroom in between and farther back down the hallway was a master bedroom with a private bathroom. And finally, at the rear of the house was a laundry room.

Nothing about the house was fancy, but it was well-loved and cared for. And Liam couldn't help but notice all of the detailed woodwork.

Of course, there were things like some of the flooring needed replacing, both bathrooms needed updating, and the kitchen could use some TLC, but it wasn't overwhelming. And best of all, they could live in it while he slowly made his way through the renovations.

As they peered out the back door at the snow-covered porch where Liam could envision sitting and watching his son play in the backyard, he didn't even have to ask Mel what she thought. The broad smile on her face said it all. Still, he had to be certain. "Think I should get it?"

Immediately she nodded. "Definitely."

"That's what I was thinking." He picked up Tate. "What do you think? Could you live here?"

"Where are the toys?"

Both Liam and Mel let out a laugh before Liam said, "They'll be here soon enough."

"What do you think?" Madison asked with a twinkle of hope in her eyes.

He glanced over at Mel, who smiled and nodded. Then he turned back to Madison. "I think it's sold."

"Perfect." Madison moved her finger over her digital notebook. "I knew as soon as I saw the place that it'd be perfect for you and your son. Now we need to talk about how much you're willing to offer. I have some papers on the kitchen island we'll need to go over."

Mel held out her hands to take Tate for him. His son seemed eager to go to her. As she talked to Tate, Liam followed the real estate agent to the kitchen—his soon-to-be kitchen. At last he was going to have his very own place.

He couldn't wait to fill this house with happy memories. He stopped to glance into the living room with its fireplace and big windows. Next year he could imagine a big Christmas tree in the corner of the room.

His gaze strayed over to where Tate and Mel sat down on the hardwood floor. His son pushed his little monster truck across the floor to Mel. He told Mel to roll it back, and she did. It was so easy to imagine them as a family.

His heart stilled at the thought. He'd sworn after his divorce that he was never getting married again. But there was something about Mel that had him seeing life differently. Maybe he just needed another chance to get things right.

It was turning out to be a great day.

Melinda was so happy for Liam to have found his forever home. It was a wonderful house, and she could imagine him spending many hours on those big porches. There was even a porch swing at the far end of the front porch, just perfect for sipping tea and saying hello to neighbors as they walked by.

But then her imagining changed from just Liam sitting alone on the porch to him sitting with a woman. They were laughing and holding hands. And then she imagined Tate stepping onto the porch followed by a younger sibling. The image caused her stomach to take a nauseous lurch.

Melinda knew it was inevitable. Liam was incredibly handsome. He was sweet and thoughtful. He was easy to be around. It was unavoidable that he would find someone to share his life with and when he did, she knew their friendship would diminish.

She just couldn't imagine her life without him in it. She looked forward to their time together. She loved to make him smile and to hear the deep rumble of his laughter. Her life would be a lot lonelier without him in it.

"Melinda, did you hear me?"

Melinda blinked and looked up at Ava. "I'm sorry. What did you say?"

"I just locked up. I'm going to take off unless you need something."

Melinda shook her head. "I'm good. Hope you have a good evening."

"You too."

Melinda had plans that evening with Liam and Tate. She wanted to celebrate him buying a house. Liam refused. He said celebrating so soon would jinx things, but she convinced him that a little celebration wouldn't hurt anything.

They were going to grab some dinner and then head out to the Apple Blossom Farm for sled riding and a bonfire. She checked the time. It was time to head out. They were meeting at the Purple Guppy for burgers before heading out to the farm, and Liam had insisted on picking her up. She refused to acknowledge how closely their plans resembled a real date.

Dinner went fine. Tate was quite chatty as his father had bought him a new truck to celebrate them finding a new house, and Tate loved the miniature fire truck. Liam had to threaten to take it away so Tate would stop playing with it long enough to eat his fries and chicken nuggets.

When they arrived at the farm, there were flood lights set up near the hill. It was abuzz with sleds and bundled-up people having a great time. Liam pulled one red plastic sled from the back of his cart and one large inner tube.

He held them both up. "Which one do you want?"

There was no hesitation on Melinda's part. "I want the inner tube."

"You've got it." Once she took it from him, he looked down at Tate. "You and I have the red one. Are you ready to sled ride?"

"Yeah!" Tate took off running toward the hill.

"Tate! Wait." Tate stopped and looked back, but he didn't retrace his steps.

"I think someone is anxious." Melinda smiled.

"You noticed that, huh?"

"Uh-huh. We better get going."

They took turns riding the inner tube. Even though the tube went faster than the sled, she found she enjoyed riding the sled with Tate more than riding the tube alone. It was so much fun to see the world through a child's eyes.

After tromping up the hillside several times, Melinda was ready for a break. "You guys, go ahead. I'll just wait for you by the fire."

"We'll take a break with you," Liam said. "Huh, Tate? You want some hot cocoa, don't you?"

"I wanna sled ride." Tate's bottom lip stuck out.

"Hey, buddy, we'll ride some more, but first we'll warm up by the fire. Okay?"

Tate's head lowered as his little shoulders slumped. Oh, to be that young again. Melinda thought about taking him back up the hill, but she didn't think Liam would like her interfering when he was trying to reason with his son, so she remained quiet.

They made their way over to where they were serving the hot cocoa. Liam got a cup to share with Tate, while she got her own cup. She took a sip of the steamy chocolate. It tasted so good. And the little marshmallows weren't so bad either.

They took a seat on one of the log benches near the fire. The heat felt so good. She could just sit there the rest of the evening, but she was certain Tate would never approve of such laziness.

Once their cocoa was finished, she looked at Liam. "Shall we go again?"

"Yes!" Tate called out.

Liam gave his son one of his lopsided smiles. "I suppose."

They only made it a few steps when Becky West approached them. Her family ran West Beach Tackle Shop. There were stress lines etched upon her face and dark shadows under her eyes. On each side of her were her three young children. "I'm so glad I ran into both of you. I was hoping you'd have a moment to talk."

"Of course," Melinda said. "What can we do for you?"

"Well..." Her gaze lowered to the trampled snow. "I'm sure you heard that Peter was injured in a car accident on the mainland."

"Yes, we did," Liam said. "How's he doing?"

"It's taking longer for him to heal than we had hoped. He's still in rehab, learning to walk again."

"I'm sorry you're going through all of this." Melinda knew the accident was bad, but she didn't know it was that severe. "I can't even imagine how hard it's been on your family. What can we do to help you?"

Becky shook her head. "Nothing. We're getting by, but I heard about your arrangement with Blackwell. And...and we don't have enough to pay the rent."

"Oh, I see." Melinda worried her bottom lip. "Have you talked to Blackwell?"

She nodded. "He's threatening to evict us, and I don't know what we'd do if we lost the shop. It's our only source of income."

Melinda reached out and gripped Becky's forearm. "We'll figure something out."

Liam cleared his throat. "Maybe we could collect enough to cover this month's rent."

Becky's eyes shimmered with unshed tears. "You all are so kind, but it's more than just this month that we owe on. We owe a few months of back rent on not only the business but also our house. Between the slow business of winter and Peter's medical bills, we just don't have the money." Becky's gaze met Melinda's. "I'm so very sorry that you are caught up in this. I don't want you to lose the bookshop."

Melinda paused as the severity of this revelation sank in. She swallowed hard and then did her best to hide the tumultuous feelings that made her stomach nauseous. "None of this is your fault. Everything will work out."

"But your bookshop—"

"Is nothing for you to worry about. You've already got enough on your hands."

Just then Becky's son yanked on her arm. "Can we sled ride?"

"Yeah. We want to sled ride," chimed in another of her children.

"In a moment." Becky turned her attention back to Melinda and Liam. "I'm really so sorry about this."

"I'm so sorry about what you're going through with your husband." Melinda gave her a hug. "Tell him we're pulling for him."

"I will." And then she walked off with her children, who were already running up the hill.

Without their rent, there's no way she could save her beloved bookshop. And then a wave of guilt washed over her. Here she was worrying about her business, when Becky had not only her business in jeopardy, but they were also about to lose their home.

Melinda's heart ached for them. And on top of it all, her husband had all sorts of medical issues that they should be focused on. There had to be a way to help them.

After all, this was Bluestar Island, where neighbors pulled together in times of trouble. She had to wonder how things had gotten this bad for the Wests without someone stepping in. And then she realized that Becky was a proud woman. She had probably been hiding her problems, hoping to resolve them on her own, but now they were too big for one person. Melinda would have to give it some thought.

CHAPTER NINETEEN

3 days before Christmas...

H E STILL HADN'T HEARD a word.

Liam checked his phone every five minutes, hoping to hear his offer to buy the house had been accepted. He'd offered them the asking price for two reasons: first, it was reasonably priced as far as Bluestar houses went, and second, he couldn't afford to lose this place. It was the exact setup he needed for Tate.

And there was a third reason. When he walked through the door, it felt like home. However, he wasn't certain if it was the actual house that gave him that warm, comforting feeling or if it was having Mel and Tate with him.

The more time he spent with Mel, the harder it was getting for him to fight his growing feelings for her. And when he saw her playing with his son, it was nearly impossible. She fit in with them, like she was the missing piece of the puzzle that made his family whole.

And yet, he knew opening his heart to someone came with great risks. He'd been absolutely certain when he'd married Audrey that his life was meant to be with her. Having to admit to himself that he'd been wrong had cut him deeply. What if he was wrong again?

He couldn't let himself go through that sort of agonizing pain again. It was just too much. And now he had to watch out for Tate. He'd been just a baby when they'd divorced. Now he was growing like a weed. If Mel was to become a permanent fixture in their lives, Tate would become attached. And if his relationship with Mel ended, it wouldn't just be Liam's scarred heart that would be tattered. It would also be his son's. And that price was just too steep to pay.

It was best to hold Mel at a distance. The sooner, the better. Which was easier said than done considering he had just dropped his son off with his neighbor, who was babysitting him while Liam went caroling with Mel. He didn't even like to sing.

He couldn't carry a tune, but somehow on the way home last night from sled riding, Mel had talked him into joining her. How did she do these things? If anyone else had asked him, he would have outright refused, but Mel had this way of talking him into things he didn't want to do.

What was her magical power? Maybe it was her smile. Definitely her smile. It could light up the world and had him agreeing to most anything just so she would smile some more. Then again there were her mesmerizing eyes. It felt as though they could see straight through him—as though she could see his every secret. And even then, she never turned away from him.

Either way, she had him going caroling. Although, he'd gotten a text to meet up at the community center fifteen minutes early. What was she up to now? He was afraid to find out.

When he stepped inside the building, he noticed the holiday lights weren't lit, and everyone was standing around with their coats on, as though ready to hit the road and start singing carols. He stood at the back of the room. His gaze searched the group of people for Mel.

He finally spotted her at the front of the room. She stepped onto the stage. "Could I have everyone's attention?!"

She had to shout because the speaker system hadn't been turned on. A hush fell over the small group.

"Thank you all for being here tonight. I've been caroling since I was a little girl, and I love the whole experience. And I know it means a lot to Bluestar's shut-ins. But before we get out there and sing our hearts out, I want to mention a couple of things. As most of you know, Peter West is still in physical rehab. While he's recovering, his family is struggling. They might lose their shop and their home. It'd be great if we could help them."

A murmur filled the room.

"Since there isn't going to be a hospital," a woman in the back shouted, "can we take the bingo money and give it to them?"

"It's a great idea. And it's one I had last night. But I spoke with Aster, and the money raised for the hospital needs to be used to expand the island's medical facility. So, we need to come up with another idea."

"A lot of us don't have any extra money," Summer Turner said. "Thanks to Blackwell raising our rent."

"I understand." Melinda nodded her head. "Maybe we can think outside of the box. If you have an idea, let me know. And now onto the second thing. Mr. Blackwell is going to be released from the hospital any day now."

"Who cares?"

Melinda ignored the outburst.

A murmur rippled through the crowd. "He's refusing to go to rehab. Instead, he's coming home."

Liam couldn't understand why she was still entangling herself with that man. Hadn't he already caused her enough trouble? And now with the Wests unable to pay their debts to Blackwell, there was no hope of Mel keeping the bookshop.

"I was hoping a couple of you would join me tomorrow to help clean up his place before he arrives home. We could make up a bedroom for him on the main floor."

"Why would we do that?" a male voice called out.

Mel didn't hesitate when she responded, "Because it's the holiday season and a chance for us to show him some good will."

"He never shows us any good will!"

"Yeah!"

Mel nodded. "I understand. And I can't argue with you, so I won't. I just wanted to put it out there that I would be at the Blackwell mansion tomorrow morning. If anyone has time to stop by and help, it would be greatly appreciated. But enough of that. Thank you for coming out tonight. It's going to be a great evening. Let's get on with the caroling."

As Mel stepped off of the stage, another murmur went through the crowd. Liam looked around. No one seemed thrilled with the idea of helping a man who was nothing but mean and nasty to all of them. If he was alone with no one to lean on in his time of need, all he had to do was look in the mirror, and he'd find the person responsible for that situation.

He didn't understand Mel's need to help the man. Liam stuffed his frustration down inside as he joined her to go caroling. He told himself to leave the subject alone. He didn't want to do anything to ruin this evening for her.

This evening was just what she needed.

Melinda had sung her heart out as they'd made their way along the streets of Bluestar. Since there were enough of them, they'd broken up into smaller groups of five or six so they could visit even more houses.

She loved seeing how people's faces would light up when they found carolers on their front porches. Their outside lights would come on, and then the door would open wide, and then the smiles would bloom on their faces.

It helped fill in the cracks in her heart. The thought of losing her bookshop cut her deep. She had absolutely no backup plan. She had no idea what she would do for work. The bookshop had been her whole world for the past six years since she'd opened it.

The thought of closing the Seaside Bookshop was just so inconceivable to her that she'd never contemplated it until now. Her only hope was that this latest health scare for Blackwell would somehow change him, that he'd finally see the light and become a compassionate man, but she'd learned a long time ago not to believe in fairy tales.

She recalled the eye rolls and the shaking of heads when she'd suggested they clean up Blackwell's house. She couldn't blame them. The man was nothing but a bitter old man, and yet she couldn't sink down to his level. If she did... If she treated him differently than she would any other Bluestar neighbor who was in need, what would that say about her?

Her mother had raised her to be a compassionate person. She wondered if her mother would approve of her actions toward Blackwell or if she would think Melinda had lost her mind just like everyone else thought, including Liam.

She'd noticed that throughout the evening, he'd been unusually quiet. She didn't have to be a rocket scientist to surmise that he was upset with her too.

If someone had told her a year ago that she would be siding with Blackwell over most everyone in Bluestar, including her best friend, she would have told them they were crazy. She would never do such a thing.

But then she recalled the fear in the man's eyes and the way he'd clung to her hand. She'd never witnessed such intense distress. In that moment, he'd been utterly alone and frightened. She couldn't turn her back on him. Nor would she now that he was coming home.

After they finished singing and returned to the community center for refreshments, Liam turned to her. "I'm heading out."

"Don't you at least want something to drink after all of that singing?"

He shook his head. "I need to pick up Tate."

Part of her wanted to just let him walk away without delving into the problem between them, but the other part of her knew if they didn't talk it out now, she wouldn't get any sleep that night. And tomorrow the gap between them would grow. In time, the distance would seem insurmountable.

"Liam, just say it."

His gaze rose to meet hers. "Say what?"

"I know you don't agree with me helping out Blackwell."

He shrugged. "If you wanted to help anyone else, I could see it. But this is the guy that fired me, and he's about to take away your bookshop. I just... I have a hard time turning off my feelings and treating him like a friend."

Her gaze searched his. "But if we don't show him compassion, are we any better than him?"

"I can't believe you said that. Now you think I'm no better than him. Yet I've been here for you through it all. I've cheered you on. And I... Never mind."

She reached out to him, but he pulled away. "Liam, that isn't what I meant."

His eyes flashed with anger. "It's what I heard. That unless I help that curmudgeon, then I'm just like him. But I don't go around raising rents sky-high. I don't fire people. And I sure don't kick tenants out of their stores."

"You aren't hearing me. I just think if I don't help him, that it says more about me than it does about him."

"So since I refuse to help tomorrow, now I'm a bad person." He shook his head. "Whatever. I have to pick up Tate."

"Liam, wait." She called out as he continued toward the door.

She wanted to go after him, but she didn't know what to say in that moment to make things better. It felt as though everything that came out of her mouth was the wrong thing to say.

Maybe she didn't know Liam as well as she'd thought. And maybe the feelings the mistletoe kiss had evoked in her didn't go both ways. The acknowledgment made her heart ache. Maybe it was better if their relationship cooled off before they ended up hurting each other even more.

CHAPTER TWENTY

2 Days before Christmas...

THIS WAS THE CRAZIEST idea ever...

Melinda arrived early the next morning with a bucket, rags, and cleaner in hand. She honestly didn't expect anyone to show up, and she couldn't blame them. Blackwell had done absolutely nothing to earn their goodwill. In fact, he'd done quite the opposite.

As she made her way onto the porch, she wondered if she should even be here. She thought about the argument she'd had with Liam the prior evening and how he'd looked at her like she'd lost her mind by suggesting doing something nice for Blackwell.

And what did she hope to accomplish by showing up here? Quite honestly she wanted to believe that she was doing it for altruistic reasons, but there was this tiny part of her that wished this act of kindness would change the man—make him more compassionate. Was that even possible after a lifetime of pushing people away?

She'd stopped by the house once a day to keep an eye on the place. The spare house key was kept beneath a potted plant to the left of the door. The plant was nothing but brown and crunchy. It had been that way since her first visit, with no hope of reviving it. The ceramic crock was large and heavy. She tilted it to the side and slid her hand under it. Her fingers touched the cold metallic of a key.

Shrugging off the worries and doubts, she stepped inside. Every time she entered this place she couldn't help but notice the inch of dust on most everything and the cobwebs. Lots of cobwebs. And that meant there had to be a lot of spiders to make all of those webs. A shiver of revulsion skittered over her skin. She *hated* spiders.

Maybe this wasn't such a good idea. Maybe, in fact, it was a bad idea. All the while her gaze searched the room for any creepy crawlies. She didn't see any, but she was certain they were there. If she just looked close enough.

Creak!

The sound made her jump. She'd been so focused on finding spiders or rather avoiding the little buggers, that she hadn't even heard the footsteps on the porch.

"Sorry, dear," said a familiar female voice. "I didn't mean to cause you to jump."

She turned around and found Birdie standing in the doorway. And she wasn't alone. Behind her was a large group of people. A smile immediately pulled at Melinda's lips.

"Are you all here to help?" Her gaze took in the assortment of mops, buckets, and cleaning supplies.

"We are. You gave us all a lot to think about. We are Bluestar. We stick together. I just hope Blackwell appreciates how you've gone out of your way for him."

Melinda silently shrugged her shoulders. Now that the shock and fear had worn off, it was likely he would revert to his old ways, but it didn't keep her from hoping.

She opened the door wide, and people stepped inside. Birdie stepped up on the new stairs Liam had been installing. She handed out orders to the awaiting people. Melinda continued to smile as she watched her neighbors and friends chip in to help one of their own—even if he didn't deserve their generosity. Even her father had shown up.

She made her way to him. "What are you doing here?"

His brows drew together. "I came to help. Isn't that what you wanted?"

"Yes, but I don't want you to overdo it." She still worried about him.

"I won't." He frowned at her. "You have to realize that I'm better. I've got this. Trust me."

Birdie's voice drew their attention. They both turned to listen to Birdie's plans for today. The woman's hand came to rest on the unfinished banister. The woodwork made Melinda think of Liam. As her gaze scanned over the crowd, she realized he wasn't there. Disappointment settled over her. She knew it was asking a lot of him after the horrible way Blackwell had treated him. Or was he not there because he was still upset with her?

Refusing to let herself dwell on the rift between her and Liam, she got to work. Someone turned on some Christmas music. Melinda loved to sing along with the festive songs. They distracted her from the tedious work.

She wanted to create a bedroom for Blackwell on the main floor. As she walked around, she came to the conclusion that the only reasonable place to assemble it was his office. It was quite large, and with a little rearranging, they could fit a small bed on the one wall. It wasn't perfect, but it would do.

As she worked to rearrange the furniture, she heard the sound of motorized equipment. She peered out the window to find a group of men including her father. They were cutting back the overgrown hedges and bushes. The smile returned to her face. People would be able to see the house from the road. And Blackwell would be able to see his neighbors. He wouldn't be isolated from the community, and she couldn't help but think that was exactly what he needed.

The morning flew by. At one point, pizzas were delivered for lunch. Melinda didn't know who'd ordered them, but she was most appreciative. This was the Bluestar she knew and loved. Everyone pitching in to help a neighbor—even a cranky one. There were a lot of clucking tongues over the way Blackwell neglected his house, but to their surprise, he put things in their proper spots.

It was the dusting and vacuuming where he truly lacked.

Melinda breathed in the fresh pine scent of the cleaner as the floors were mopped. It was amazing what a small army could do to a house in a matter of hours. It didn't even look like the same place. She just hoped Blackwell would appreciate their efforts.

Buzz-buzz.

Melinda reached for her phone. When she checked the caller ID, she realized it was the harbormaster. She'd set it up with him to call her when Blackwell came home. She definitely didn't expect it to be this soon.

After she concluded the brief conversation, she moved to the unfinished staircase. "Everyone! Can I have your attention?" It took a moment for everyone to quiet down. "I've just heard that Blackwell is on the island, and he's on his way here. So, please finish up quickly."

Ten minutes later, a Bluestar TaxiCart pulled up in front of the house. Melinda rushed out onto the porch. All the while her heart pounded. She had absolutely no idea how the man was going to react to the work that had been done.

Blackwell got out with a new cane and no longer having a walking boot on his ankle. He paused at the end of the walkway and took in the cut hedges. His face was expressionless.

Everyone that had been working in the house streamed out and stood off to the side of the large covered porch. They were so quiet Blackwell's steps seemed loud. He slowly made his way up the walk.

When he reached Melinda, he asked, "What's going on?"

"We wanted to do something for your homecoming."

His bushy brows drew together. Without another word, he stepped inside to find a small artificial Christmas tree on the round table beneath the crystal chandelier in the foyer.

Melinda loved the touch of holiday flair. She wished she had thought of it. She noticed he was extremely quiet. She didn't know if that was good or bad.

As he slowly made his way around the first floor, examining each room, she followed him. She wasn't sure what to say.

When he finally made it to his office, he stopped next to the twin bed that she'd made up for him. He turned to her. "Are you responsible for all of this?"

Oh no. This was not the response she'd been hoping for. She swallowed hard. "Yes. It was my idea."

He arched a brow. "If you expect me to pay you all, you can forget it. I didn't ask for any of this."

"We don't want to be paid."

Confusion showed in his eyes. "You have to want something. No one does something like this without wanting something in return."

Melinda never met such a suspicious person. "We did this because we wanted to. You could consider it a Christmas gift from the town."

Blackwell was quiet for a moment as his gaze took in the clean room. A smile broke out on his weathered face. "Thank you. No one has ever done anything so thoughtful for me."

She smiled back at him. "But it wasn't just me. It was a lot of people from town." She started naming names. "They all wanted to help. Now you need to thank them." When he didn't move, she said, "Go on."

Blackwell turned and with a bit of a limp made his way to the porch. He cleared his throat. "Thank you all for taking time out of your day to help me." He paused as though unsure of what to say next. "Anyway, I appreciate it."

When he stepped inside, the crowd of people dispersed. Melinda couldn't make out their reaction to his words. She could only hope it was the beginning of change.

She smiled at him. "There. That wasn't so bad, was it?"

"I suppose not." His gaze met hers. "Without you, none of this would have happened. You continue to surprise me. I didn't know anyone like you existed in this world."

She glanced down as heat rushed to her cheeks. "I'm not special. It's just the Bluestar way."

"And yet I've lived here all of my life and never experienced this sort of outpouring."

Melinda wanted to make sure he knew if he didn't change his ways that things would return to the way they'd been. "If you want it to continue, if you want people in your life, you'll have to change. You'll need to become a part of the community." She understood this transformation would be hard for him, but some of the best things in life were the ones you had to work for. "I know you're used to spending all of your time alone, so I'm not asking you to be the life of the party, but be present and have a kind word for your neighbors. Amazing things can grow from the tiniest gestures."

"I...I don't know. I'm too old to change."

"No, you aren't." When he didn't look convinced, she said, "Look at how far we've come."

"But that's different—you're different."

She'd take his words as a compliment. "Just try. I think you'll be surprised."

"I'll try if you tell me what you would like in return. The one thing you'd like most this Christmas."

What would it hurt to tell him? "I would like you to rehire Liam to finish the amazing job he started."

Blackwell's eyes widened. "Are you sure that's what you want most?"

Without a single doubt, she nodded. "Yes."

"But I thought you would ask to keep your bookshop."

The thought had crossed her mind, but it wasn't as important to her as Liam. This time she didn't miss how profound this realization was for her. "I can always find another location for the bookshop. It's not the roof and walls that make it special. It's the readers who step through the door. They share with me their passion for reading and tell me how a book has touched their lives. But in the end, it's a very special friend that I can't replace. There's no one in my life like Liam. He's been there for me through thick and thin." The thought of how he didn't show up today crossed her mind, but she quickly dismissed it. "I want to help him this Christmas."

"I don't know what to say. He's a very lucky man. I hope he knows just how fortunate he is. I've never known such a special friendship."

"It's never too late to find that special friend."

Melinda gathered her things and made her way home. This evening was the Ugly Sweater Contest. She'd already worked on her sweater. It was hanging on her bedroom door. It was green, and because she was unable to forget about the mistletoe kiss with Liam, she decorated the sweater with felt mistletoe and red bows. The sleeves and waist were trimmed with white garland and gold jingle bells. It was her best work to date.

And yet her heart just wasn't up for attending the party. She decided to stay home and curl up on the couch with a blanket. She flipped through the television stations until she stumbled across *It's a Wonderful Life*. It felt rather fitting for the evening.

—— *ele* ——

Where is it?

Liam searched through his tool chest, but there was no sign of his favorite screwdriver, the one he used the most. It wasn't too big or too small. It was the perfect size to fit most every project. And he needed it right now to put together the little table he'd made Tate for Christmas.

He'd been distracted all day to the point where Tate was even giving him strange looks. Liam could blame it on his lack of sleep, but it wasn't the whole truth.

He couldn't stop thinking about his disagreement with Mel. He tried to figure out her need to help the town Scrooge to the point of alienating her friends. Maybe it had to do with the trauma of her father's heart problems. Still, he felt there was more to it.

Or maybe he hoped there was more of a reason that she'd chosen to stand by a man who didn't have one nice word to say about Liam's work and had no qualms about firing him. Liam had never been fired in his life. His pride had taken a giant blow.

And then Mel actually thought he'd brush all of that aside and show up to clean the man's house. No way! It wasn't going to happen.

He turned his thoughts back to the immediate problem. Sure he could use his power screwdriver, but the truth of the matter was that he wanted an excuse to get out of the woodshop. So, he bundled up Tate, and off they went to visit Jack.

Liam wasn't sure his brother would be home. Since his brother worked from home, he was there most of the time. But it was evening now, and there was a chance his brother had plans. The thought of going home to be alone with his thoughts didn't appeal to him. So, when Jack opened the door, Liam was relieved.

Jack's forehead scrunched up. "What are you doing here? Was I supposed to watch Tate?"

Liam shook his head. "I was doing some work at the shop, and I realized you'd borrowed my screwdriver."

His brother gave him a confused look. "You came over here for a screwdriver when you have plenty of them?"

He frowned at his brother. "Are you going to invite us in or what?"

Without a word, Jack opened the door wide. "Come on in."

Once Liam had Tate's coat off and got out some of the toys from the backpack he took everywhere with them, he sat down on the couch. It was only then he realized this wasn't where he wanted to be. He was supposed to be with Mel at the ugly sweater contest, but after the way he blew her off that day, he knew she wouldn't want anything to do with him this evening.

"How long are you going to sit on the couch, scowling?" Jack's voice interrupted his thoughts.

"I'm not scowling." Was he? Were his thoughts that transparent?

"Yes, you were. What's going on with you?"

Before Liam could brush off his brother's question, Tate ambled over. One of the wheels had come off his truck. Liam had a feeling the wheel hadn't just fallen off but rather had been pulled off by his surprisingly strong son. Tate liked to take things apart to see how they worked. It was putting everything back together that he struggled with.

Once Liam had the truck running again, he turned to his brother, who still had an expectant look on his face. "You aren't going to let this go, are you?"

"Not a chance. So, what's going on? I thought you'd be with Mel this evening."

"Why would you think that?"

"Because you've spent most of the holiday together. So, it makes me suspicious when I see you here instead of at that sweater contest with her. What gives?"

Liam sighed. He supposed he had gone there to talk, so he might as well get it over with. He filled his brother in on how Blackwell fired him before having a medical emergency, and now Mel was fixing up the curmudgeon's house.

"I just feel like she sided with him over me." Liam felt all sorts of twisted and conflicted. "And I know that's wrong because the man just had a stroke. But is this medical incident supposed to override his lifetime of meanness and greed?"

Jack was quiet for a moment, as though considering what Liam had told him. "Maybe it isn't about Blackwell."

"Of course it is. He's the one that fired me for no good reason, and now Mel is going out of her way for him."

"But maybe her act of generosity is more about overcoming his meanness with a display of kindness. Maybe she's struggling to take the high road instead of sinking to the man's low road."

"I don't know. Maybe I just don't know her as well as I thought."

Jack leaned back. "I think you know her plenty well. In fact, you might be putting up road blocks."

"What's that supposed to mean?"

"You really don't know."

Liam inwardly groaned. "Would I have asked if I did?"

Jack was quiet for a moment. "I've seen you two together, and you love her."

"I do not." The too-quick response sounded hollow even to his own ears.

Jack continued as though Liam hadn't spoken. "I think you love her, and it scares you. You've already had one failed relationship, and you're afraid to take another chance. And so you think you can keep her as your friend, but sometimes even that doesn't work. When you feel yourself getting too close to her, you throw on the brakes."

"And this is me braking?" When Jack nodded, Liam thought it over. He realized his little brother just might be on to something. "Since when did you become so wise?"

"Shh... Don't let that get out. I don't have time to hand out advice to everyone."

Liam let out a laugh. "Don't worry. I don't think anyone will believe me."

"Hey! That's not funny." Jack frowned at him.

It didn't stop Liam from laughing. It felt good to laugh. He'd been frowning way too much since he'd had words with Mel. Now he had to do something about patching things up with her. But what? He knew it had to be something big.

Chapter Twenty-One

Christmas Eve

*H*OW WAS IT THE *day before Christmas already?*

Liam wasn't ready for the big day. It didn't help that he'd had another restless night. He'd spent a great deal of it tossing and turning. He'd heard what his brother said. Was he subconsciously sabotaging his relationship with Mel?

With a string of yawns that morning, he'd downed half a pot of coffee. Somehow he just had to fix things with Mel today. He couldn't imagine spending Christmas with Mel mad at him.

At last, a possible solution came to him. It would be a way for him to show Mel just how much she meant to him. It would be perfect for her. However, this plan also came with a steep price. It would mean giving up something important to him. And he had no guarantee it would work. He didn't let that stop him.

With it nearing lunchtime, he headed over to his parents' place. They'd returned home the night before. When he arrived, he expected them to be frantically rushing around, but to his utter surprise, they had their holiday plans well in hand.

He wasn't sure if he'd ever be as organized as them. They even had their gifts wrapped before they'd left to visit with his aunt and uncle.

When his mother had offered to spend some time with Tate, Liam had jumped on the offer. It would give him a chance to put his win-Mel-back plan into action.

First, he made a call to the real estate agent. It was with the deepest regret that he would have to pull out of the offer to buy the house. He told himself it was a small price to pay in order to win back the woman that he'd come to love.

His body tensed. It was the first time he'd admitted he loved her. As the four-letter word rolled around in his mind, the surprise wore away and acceptance settled in. He loved Mel.

And if giving up the house would help heal things between them, he would do it. After all, there would be other houses. Maybe they wouldn't be as perfect as this one, but he'd make them work.

With his plan underway, he set off with a specific destination in mind. He drove by the Seaside Bookshop and was surprised to see a red and white banner that read: *Going out of business sale*! His heart sank. He knew how much Mel loved the place. And she wasn't the only one. The people of Bluestar frequented it. Even his young son was falling in love with books.

He wanted to stop and tell her to take down the banner, but he couldn't do it. He couldn't get her hopes up until he spoke to Blackwell.

He tramped on the accelerator. He was a man on a mission. A couple of minutes later, he pulled to a stop in front of Blackwell's house. The truth of the matter was he'd almost passed up the place because it looked totally different.

The hedges and bushes had been cut down and shaped. They weren't even waist-high now. It gave the passerby a clear view of the Blackwell mansion. Mel had certainly gone out of her way to take the high road where Blackwell was concerned. Liam just hoped the man appreciated all she'd done for him.

Liam made his way up the walkway. There were lights on inside the house. When he stepped onto the edge of the porch, the door swung open, and there stood Blackwell with no cast or crutches. The only thing he had to aid him was a cane.

"What are you doing here?" Blackwell's bushy brows were knitted together. "It's Christmas Eve."

It wasn't the friendliest greeting, but he hadn't threatened to have him arrested for trespassing, so that was something. "Could we speak?"

"If this is about your job—"

"It's not."

Blackwell hesitated before opening the door wide enough to allow Liam to enter. When Liam stepped inside the house, he was blown away by all of the changes. The place didn't just look clean; it smelled it too. There wasn't an inch of dust on the table in the foyer. And the chandelier was so much brighter without the cobwebs and dust. In the center of the wooden table, with the beautiful inlaid geometric pattern, was a miniature Christmas tree. And the little tree lights were lit—meaning Blackwell had turned them on.

"You wanted to discuss something." Blackwell's voice drew Liam from perusing all of the changes to the house.

Liam cleared his throat. "Yes." He reached into his pocket and withdrew a check. "This is for you."

Blackwell took the check and stared at it. "What's this for?"

"This will pay for the Wests' back rent and in the process, it means Mel gets to keep her bookshop. Her obligation to you has been fulfilled and by the deadline."

"But how did you come up with so much money?"

"It doesn't matter. All that matters is that you don't evict anyone. Agreed?"

"You must have had to sacrifice something to come up with this much cash." Blackwell's curious gaze poked and prodded Liam.

He shook his head. "It doesn't matter. It was worth it. I would do anything for Mel."

"So you aren't here about your job?"

"No. Why would I be?"

"You didn't talk to Melinda?"

"No. Why?" He felt as though something big had happened, and he was the last to know.

"I shouldn't have fired you. If you want, you can have your job back." He moved to his desk and returned with a check. "Here's the balance of what I owe you plus a bonus for such detailed work."

Liam hesitated as Blackwell held the check out to him. It was hard to believe his own ears. Blackwell had apologized and complimented his work. Who said Christmas miracles didn't happen? Or was this all thanks to Mel and her insistence on showing the man compassion? Or maybe it was a little bit of both.

"Go ahead and take it." Blackwell waved the check at him. "I promise they'll honor it at the bank."

He accepted the check and was shocked by the four-figure bonus that was included. "I don't understand."

"You've got a really good friend watching out for you. Never take them for granted."

Liam stared him in the eyes. "You're talking about Mel, aren't you?"

He nodded. "I asked her what she wanted most for Christmas. I thought for sure she'd ask for the bookshop, but she said she can replace it, but she could never replace her relationship with you. You two deserve each other. I mean that in a good way."

At last things were going his way. Liam was anxious to go to her—to tell her that she could take down that going out of business sign. He thought of her smiling at him—of her hugging him. At last, they'd be back on track, and then he could tell her how he felt about her.

And yet he hesitated. Even though he didn't regret spending his down payment on the bookshop, he realized he didn't want Mel to feel indebted to him. That wasn't the way he wanted to win her over. And it certainly wasn't the circumstances he wanted to use to win her over.

His gaze met Blackwell's. "Will you tell her about the bookshop?"

Blackwell's eyes clouded with confusion. "You don't want to tell her?"

Liam shook his head. "It would be better coming for you."

He sighed. "I'll never understand young people. Yes, I'll tell her."

"Thank you." Liam turned for the door before pausing to turn back. "Merry Christmas. I'll start working again after Christmas."

"Why don't you wait until after the New Year?"

Liam hesitated. "Are you sure?"

"It was my idea, wasn't it?" Blackwell quipped.

"Of course. See you then."

Liam rushed out the door, stunned by the change in Blackwell. He certainly wasn't the same man that had hired him. That man didn't know how to smile or have any kindness. All of that had changed.

Most people would probably write off the change due to his health scare. That would probably change most people. But Liam couldn't help but wonder if it was Mel's kindness that had led Blackwell down this path to becoming a decent human being—a likable person. 'Tis the season for miracles, both big and small. He hoped there was room for one more—for Mel to give him a second chance.

She had been wrong.

Melinda had tried to talk positively about losing her bookshop. She'd really tried to be strong, but the truth was she'd been fighting tears all day. She'd nearly broken down when she'd hung the going-out-of-business sign in front of the bookshop.

She wasn't going to go through with the sale, but she'd rather slash prices and profits to get the books into readers' hands than box them up and store them until she found another storefront. She had absolutely no idea when that might be. It certainly wouldn't be the same as this place, which felt like her second home.

The last thing she wanted to do was go out that day, but it was Christmas Eve. Today was the community dinner. It was an early meal at five o'clock, giving everyone a chance to get home early to make their preparations for the big day.

She would have canceled her plans except for the fact that she'd made a big deal about it to her father. He wasn't going to go, but she'd insisted. He'd finally relented. And now it was her who didn't want to go and see all of the sympathy in her friends' eyes. It would just make the pain of the situation that much worse for her.

She pulled to a stop in front of her father's house, which was her childhood home. Usually, when they were going somewhere together, he would be waiting for her at the doorway, but he was nowhere to be seen.

She got out and rushed to the door because it was starting to snow. She'd heard something about a white Christmas in the forecast. She just hadn't caught how much was in store for them.

She knocked and then let herself inside. "Dad? Are you ready to go?"

"Back here," he called from the kitchen. It had always been the hub of the house when she was growing up.

In her memories, her mother always had the house smelling good from homemade bread to soups and roasts. Her mother was a remarkable cook. To this day, Melinda still missed her mother's cooking.

She stepped into the kitchen to find her father sitting at the table with a cup of what she hoped was decaf coffee. He wasn't supposed to have caffeine since his episode this past summer.

"Hey, Dad. Are you ready to go? We don't want to be late."

He lifted his gaze to meet hers. "I stopped by the bookshop to see you today."

"You did? I didn't see you." She also hadn't told him about the going-out-of-business sale. She just couldn't bring herself to do it. By admitting it to him, it would make it oh so real to her—the same way the sale today had driven home the reality of what was happening.

"Why didn't you tell me?"

She shrugged. "There was no reason to worry you."

His gaze searched hers. "But I could have helped."

She shook her head. "This is my problem."

"And you are my daughter. Don't you know that I would do anything for you?"

His words touched her heart. "And I would do anything for you. I didn't tell you because I didn't want you getting upset. It's not good for your heart."

He got to his feet. "My heart is fine. When are you going to believe it?"

This conversation had been a long time in coming. She'd put it off at every turn, but it seemed as though today was her day to face all of the difficult things in her life.

"You don't understand," she said. "I... I had to see you in that hospital bed. I didn't know if you were going to live or die. It ranked right up there with losing Mom as one of the worst times of my life. I can't go through that again." Her voice wobbled with emotion. "I can't lose you."

"Oh, sweetie. You aren't going to lose me." Her father moved to her and wrapped her in one of his bear hugs. And in the moment, she let the tears flow that she'd been holding back all day.

She didn't know how much time passed when she pulled herself together and straightened. She swiped at her cheeks. "I'm sorry. It's been a rough day."

"And that's why I want to give you the money to keep the bookshop open." When she went to speak, he held up his hand. "I've done a lot of thinking, and I think your mother would be in agreement. I have some savings, and you're welcome to it."

"Oh, Dad, that's so sweet of you, but I can't take it."

"Yes, you can. I insist."

She shook her head. "You don't understand. I need to do this my way. It'll all work out."

His brows scrunched up together. "How?"

"I don't know yet. I'll find another shop to rent. It might take me a little time, but I'll figure something out. You should take that money and travel."

"I can't. I have to work."

"You could retire."

This time it was him who shook his head. "It's not going to happen, at least not any time in the near future." His concerned gaze met hers. "Are you sure you won't take the money?"

"I'm positive. But thank you. I've got this."

"Well, if you won't take it, it'll be here if you ever need to borrow it."

"I appreciate it. Now we should get going so we can get some dinner."

"Speaking of which. I have cheesy potatoes in the oven. You know, the kind your mother used to make, or at least as close to her recipe as I could get them."

"Sounds delicious." It was a dish her mother used to make for special occasions. "And I made her macaroni salad."

He smiled. "Can't wait to have some."

"Then we better get going."

While her father gathered his things, she touched up her makeup. It wasn't perfect, but it was good enough. And then they were out the door as the snowflakes continued to lightly fall.

CHAPTER TWENTY-TWO

A FEW MINUTES LATER, they were at the community center. The place was bustling with people all dressed up for the holiday, carrying pans and bowls of food. This was going to be a delicious covered-dish feast with the town kicking in the roast beef and fried chicken catered by the Lighthouse Café.

With white twinkle lights glowing overhead, Melinda arranged the dishes of food on one of the long banquet tables lined with a red tablecloth. Even though her heart was heavy with the thought of losing her bookshop, she was not going to let it ruin the evening. She didn't lose sight of the fact that she had her father to spend Christmas with. And after almost losing him that summer, this holiday together was a miracle—one she wouldn't take lightly.

She felt a tap on her shoulder. Her heart immediately beat faster. She willed it to be Liam standing behind her. She had so much she wanted to say to him. The fact they were at odds with each other weighed heavy on her.

When she turned, she was disappointed. "Mr. Blackwell. I... I didn't expect to see you here."

"Truth be told, I didn't expect to be here myself either. If this were a couple of weeks ago, I wouldn't have considered being her, but a lot of things have changed for me this Christmas. Thanks in part to you."

"Me?" She pressed a hand to her chest.

He nodded. "You showed me that I don't have to be alone—that there is something more important than money."

She couldn't believe these words were coming from the town curmudgeon. She supposed after this Christmas, they wouldn't be able to call him that any longer. "What's more important?"

"Friends like you." He smiled at her. "And there's one other thing..."

"What's that?"

"You need to take down that going-out-of-business sign."

"Oh." She hadn't realized the sign would be a problem. "I'm sorry. It won't be up for long. I just hoped to sell off some more books after Christmas. Then I'll take it down."

He shook his head. "You misunderstand me. You need to take down the sign because you aren't going out of business."

"I'm not?" She was confused. "But our agreement... Wait. Did you change your mind? Is that why I get to keep the bookshop? Thank you so much!"

"It wasn't me. I never got the chance to change my mind because I had a visitor who paid everything that was owed on our agreement."

"A visitor?" Who would have that kind of money? It wasn't her father as he would have told her. So then who was it?

"It was Liam."

Her mouth opened, but no words came out. She turned. Her gaze searched through the growing crowd of festively dressed people. She didn't see him. *Please let him be here.*

Then realizing that Blackwell was still at her side, she turned back to him. "I'm sorry, but I really need to speak to Liam if I can find him."

"Don't worry. I have a feeling he'll be here."

"Thank you. Merry Christmas."

"Merry Christmas to you too."

She slowly made her way through the crowd. She paused to ask Sara if she'd seen Liam. She hadn't. She asked Aster and then her father. No one had seen Liam. Where was he?

She stopped working her way through the crowd. She realized all she had to do was call him. She reached into her purse and pulled out her phone. His number was the last one called. She hit redial. The phone rang and rang before switching to voicemail.

"Liam, I need to talk to you."

"I need to talk to you too." His voice didn't come from the phone but rather from behind her.

She spun around to see Liam standing there. His face was devoid of expression, so she had absolutely no idea what he was thinking.

She glanced around. "Where's Tate?"

Liam gestured to the other side of the room. "He's with his grandparents. I thought it would give us a moment to talk."

Her heart pitter-pattered. What did he want to talk about? She knew there was something she needed to say first. She searched for the right words to say to him. And then she uttered the words from her heart.

"I'm sorry." They both uttered the words at the same time.

She gaped at him. And then they both smiled. In that moment, she felt as though she'd gotten her friend back. Was it possible they could share something more? She hoped so. She wanted to spend many more Christmases together.

First, she needed to understand his actions. "Why did you do it? Why did you pay Blackwell the back rent?"

"I wanted to help the Wests. When I told them, they insisted they would pay me back. I told them there was no rush. Becky looked so relieved. I didn't do it just for them. I did it for me too."

"For you?"

He nodded. "I couldn't let the Seaside Bookshop go out of business because it's my favorite bookstore. And I happen to think the owner is very special."

Her heart skipped a beat. What was he trying to tell her? Did he care about her too?

She halted her thoughts. She was jumping too far ahead. "But where did you get the money?" As she spoke the words, the answer came to her.

"You used the downpayment for the house, didn't you?"

"Yes."

"Why did you do it? Why would you give up on the house? It was perfect for the two of you."

"The timing wasn't right."

She didn't believe him. "Of course it's the right time. You've been looking for months for just the right place. And you know with the housing shortage that it isn't easy. It's not too late. Get the money back and get the house."

He shook his head. "I'm not taking back the money. It not only helps you, but it helps the West family."

"You're right. They really need the help. I'm just so sorry about the house."

He stared deep into her eyes. "Don't you know by now that I would do anything for you?"

Her pulse raced. These were the words she'd been longing to hear. She stepped closer to him and tilted her chin upward until their gazes met. "And I would do anything for you."

"As in getting my job back at Blackwell's?" When she didn't say anything, he continued. "He told me he offered you one wish for Christmas, and you didn't pick the bookshop." He reached out to her and drew her even closer. "Instead, you wanted me to get my job back."

Her hands landed on his chest. "I felt bad about drawing you into my problems. It wasn't fair that you lost your job, especially when you were doing such an amazing job." Her hands slid up over his broad shoulders and wrapped around the back of his neck.

His voice lowered. "You like my work, huh?"

"I do. I really do."

"Then wait until you see what I do next." His gaze moved to her lips.

The breath stilled in her lungs. He was going to kiss her. She'd longed for this moment ever since their mistletoe kiss. As he lowered his head toward her, her eyelids fluttered shut. She lifted up on her tiptoes to meet him in the middle.

His warm lips pressed to hers. There was something different about this kiss—something much deeper. Maybe it was because at last she was willing to admit what was right there in front of her all along—her love for him.

As they kissed, her feet felt as though they were floating on a cloud. Her heart beat so hard it echoed in her ears. She wondered if he could feel her heartbeat. Did he know how he affected her?

When he pulled back, it took her a moment to come back down to earth. She blinked and met his gaze. What exactly did this kiss mean to him?

Her gaze searched his. "Why did you pay Blackwell?"

"I told you."

"No. What motivated you to do something so grand?" She needed to hear him say the words.

"Don't you know? Isn't it obvious?" With her heart lodged in her throat, she couldn't speak, so he continued. "I love you. I think I've loved you since last summer when you insisted we work together on a reading nook for your bookshop."

Her heart leaped with joy as a smile pulled at the corners of her lips. "I love you too. I've loved you since you insisted on sitting at the hospital with me day after day until my father was out of ICU. No one had ever done something like that for me. I knew then and there that you were different from any other man I've ever known. And your most amazing little boy has charmed his way into my heart."

"I think it goes both ways. He adores you too."

They kissed again but were quickly interrupted when Mayor Banks stepped up on the stage. "Ladies and gentlemen, can I have your attention?"

With their hands clasped and their fingers laced together, they turned to the stage. Melinda couldn't stop smiling. This was the best Christmas ever.

"Welcome to Bluestar's community Christmas Eve dinner," Mayor Banks said. "Thank you for all of the amazing food you brought. I can't wait to start sampling it. I might need two or three plates since there's so much." As the mayor continued to talk, Melinda leaned her head against Liam's muscled shoulder.

"Excuse me, Mayor." Blackwell stepped onto the stage. "May I say a few words?"

"I... Uh..." For once Mayor Banks looked totally caught off guard. "Okay..."

The mayor stepped off to the side while Blackwell moved to the microphone. He cleared his throat as though he were uncomfortable to be standing in front of so many people. "I want to thank many of you that came to my place and took the house and made it back into a home. I'm humbled by your outpouring of generosity. I realize that I don't deserve it, and that's what makes it so special."

Melinda couldn't believe Blackwell had made such a profound transformation. She was so proud of him. Who said old dogs can't learn new tricks? Blackwell was proving them wrong. Go him!

"There are two people in this room that have shown me the true meaning of Christmas. And it wasn't anything they did for me. It was the way they were willing to sacrifice what was most important to them for the sake of the other. I've never seen such caring and devotion. They have shown me the true meaning of Christmas."

Tears pricked the back of Melinda's eyes as she realized he was talking about Liam and herself. She blinked repeatedly before glancing up at Liam. He was looking at her. He realized who Blackwell was speaking of too.

"For the first time in my life," Blackwell said, "I feel as though I am a part of this community. And I know I have a lot to make up for. I plan to work on that, starting with donating money to the hospital fund." Applause echoed through the room. When it died down, he said, "For those of you that rent from me, you can forget about the rent increase."

Cheers and whistles rippled through the room. Both Melinda and Liam joined in the applause. This was huge.

When the room quieted down once more, Blackwell said, "Instead of a hike in the rent, I'll be lowering everyone's rent by twenty-five percent."

Another cheer roared through the room as Blackwell backed away from the microphone. Mayor Banks stepped up and invited everyone to enjoy the delicious feast.

Melinda turned back to Liam. "Can you believe that?"

"Miracles really do happen. And there's another one in the works." He nodded off in the distance.

"What are you talking about?" She glanced around but wasn't sure what he was looking at.

"Your father and my aunt are talking."

"What's so special about that?"

He pointed them out. They were laughing and making direct eye contact. "I haven't seen your father that happy since before he went to the hospital. Have you?"

She studied her father. There was definitely a spark in his eyes, and he was animated as though he were truly enjoying himself. "No. I haven't."

"Hm… My aunt just moved to the island over the summer. She's a widow. Maybe it's the beginning of something."

Melinda gently elbowed him. "Liam, they hardly know each other."

He turned to her and rested his hands on her hips. "People could have said the same thing about us this past summer and now look at us."

She rested her palms on his chest, feeling the steady beat of his heart. "People would now say that I'm crazy in love with you."

"They'd say the same about me. I love you with all of my heart. Merry Christmas."

"Merry Christmas." She lifted up on her tiptoes and pressed her lips to his.

It was the best Christmas ever.

EPILOGUE

Three months later...

L IFE COULDN'T BE ANY better.

Liam couldn't stop smiling. Everything was going right, even the weather was cooperating. March weather had come in like a lamb. The sun was shining, and it was unseasonably warm out. It was hard to imagine it was still technically winter.

Liam opened the door of the real estate office for Mel. With a big smile on both of their faces, they stepped outside. Lots of people were out and about, enjoying the spring-like weather.

Mel stopped and turned to him. "You did it. You own the house."

He wanted to say that they'd done it together because she'd been by his side through this whole adventure. And yet he realized it was just his name on the mortgage. He wondered if Mel had wished they'd officially bought the house together.

It wouldn't be long until they made all of the big decisions together because he had another proposal in the works. A ring box burned a hole in his pocket. Every time he'd intended to ask Mel to marry him, there had been an interruption, from

Tate having a cold and needing extra cuddles to a broken water pipe at the bookshop. Luckily, the leak had been in the back of the store and hadn't damaged the books.

But today everything was going great. And he wasn't going to let it end now. "Let's go to lunch to celebrate."

"Oh, yeah. Sure. I'm so happy for you." When she smiled at him like that, it made his heart skip a beat.

He took her hand in his. It felt so natural for her fingers to be entwined with his. "Where would you like to go?"

She shrugged. "This is your celebration. You should pick."

"This is *our* celebration. *We* did this together."

He saw the look on her face—the one that said this was his house not hers—but she didn't utter the words. "How about we go to the Lighthouse Café? I would love one of their chocolate milkshakes."

He leaned forward and gave her a quick kiss. "Me too. Let's go."

They'd opted to walk and soak up some of the sunshine. And so, they set off for the restaurant. For a while, they walked in companionable silence.

She glanced over at him. "And here I thought you'd want to go straight to the new house to start cleaning so you can get moved in right away."

"We have plenty of time for that, but right now I think a celebration is in order." In front of the café, he stopped and turned to her. When she sent him a questioning gaze, he asked, "Do you have any idea how much I love you?"

"As much as I love you."

He shook his head. "More."

"No. I love you more." She smiled at him as they'd had this disagreement many times.

"I love you the most." He wasn't giving up. He needed her to know just how much he cared about her.

"I love you the most-est."

"That's not a word."

"It is now. I win." She grinned at him.

"No. I win." He withdrew the black ring box from his pocket, and then he dropped to one knee. He opened the box and held it up to her.

Mel's big brown eyes opened wide. She audibly gasped. She pressed a hand to her mouth.

People on the sidewalk stopped to watch them. He hadn't planned to do this in front of an audience, but he'd waited long enough. He'd come to the conclusion that no time was going to be perfect. But when they'd started their debate over who loved the other the most, it felt as close to perfect as he would get.

"Melinda Coleman, I have loved you for what feels like forever, and in other ways it feels like our story has just begun. You bring out the best in me and make me want to strive to be a better man." He watched as the happy tears streamed down her cheeks. "Life is an adventure, and I'm hoping you'll go on that adventure with me. Will you marry me?"

"Yes." She was nodding and crying...and smiling through it all. "Yes, I will."

He pulled the ring from the box and slipped it onto her finger.

"Wait!" a female voice called out.

What in the world? Someone wanted to crash their engagement? Wasn't that supposed to be at the wedding when they ask if anyone objects? Who objects to an engagement?

His head swiveled around, searching for the person behind the voice. It certainly wasn't one of his exes. He hadn't dated anyone after his divorce, except Mel.

When he spotted a woman whom he'd never seen before approaching them, he called out. "What do you want?"

With Liam still on bended knee, the woman said, "Can I take your photo?"

They both glanced over at the woman. She had straight brown hair that brushed over her shoulders. Around her neck she wore a strap attached to a camera. She had a pleasant enough smile with an eager gleam in her eyes.

When he went to straighten, the woman said, "Don't move. It's a perfect shot with you right there."

He remained kneeling as he glanced up at his bride. Mel shrugged. Obviously she didn't know the woman either.

"I'll make sure you get a copy," the woman said.

"Why do you want our photo?" he asked.

"Because it's small-town love. It's perfect. People will love the story—your story." She stopped as though she knew she was getting ahead of herself. "My name's Elaine Dell, but people call me Lainey." She spoke quickly as though worried about getting cut off before she could get it all out there. "I'm a travel blogger, and this would be great for a story. But even if you don't want your story published, I'd still be willing to take the photo for you."

Not planning to stay in this position much longer, he said to Mel, "It's okay with me. What do you think?"

Mel nodded her head.

"Go ahead," he said to Lainey. "Do you want me to stay here?"

"Yes." The young woman started to back up. "Can you take her hand in yours and stare up at her?"

He did as the woman asked. He hoped the woman knew how to take a good photograph. It would make a nice keepsake.

"Stay right there. I just need to move over..."
Thunk!

A scream tore through the air. Liam glanced over to see the woman lying in the road. A cart was right next to her. Had she been hit?

Liam's gaze lifted to see his brother Jack sitting behind the wheel of the cart. His brother was pale with a horrified look on his face. The woman was still on the ground. She slowly sat up, looking a bit dazed.

Jack leaped out of the cart and rushed to her side. "Are you okay?"

"I... I don't know." The woman's hair was mussed up, and there was a little bit of blood on her temple.

"I'll call 9-1-1." Jack reached for his phone.

"No. Don't." There was a firmness in the woman's voice mixed with a bit of panic. "I'm fine."

When she went to stand, her face creased. Oh no! This wasn't good. Not good at all.

Keep reading Melinda and Liam's story! Sign up for my newsletter and receive not one but TWO bonus scenes:

Get your bonus epilogue HERE.

And read about Aster and Sam Bell's Christmas baby HERE.

Then return to Bluestar Island for the next book in this heartwarming series... A LIGHTHOUSE SNAPSHOT. Continue reading the bumpy start to Elaine "Lainey" and Jack's story. And keep up with Harvey Coleman as he gets to know Jack's aunt better. Maybe it's never too late for a second chance at love... A lot is going on as springtime blooms on Bluestar Island!

SANTA'S MITTENS COOKIES

(makes 24)

INGREDIENTS:

¾ cup dark brown sugar
¾ cup unsalted butter, softened
½ tsp baking powder
¼ tsp salt
2 tsp vanilla
1 egg
2 ¼ cups flour
1 cup pecans
4 oz white chocolate baking bar
White sanding sugar
Red sanding sugar

- Preheat oven to 300°F

- Spread pecans on lined baking sheet. Bake 8 mins.

- Let cool and then chop them.

- Combine butter and dark brown sugar. Mix.

- Add baking powder, salt, and vanilla. Mix.

- Add egg. Mix.

- Slowly add flour, a little at a time. Mix just until moistened.

- Add pecans. Stir by hand until combined.

- If dough is too soft/sticky, add one tablespoon of flour.

- Chill dough in fridge, one to two hours.

- Preheat oven to 350°F

- Line baking sheet with parchment paper.

- On a lightly floured surface, roll half the dough to an ¼ inch thickness.

- Use mitten-shaped cookie cutter to cut out cookies.

- Place on parchment paper.

- Sprinkle finger portion of mitten with red sanding sugar.

- Bake 12-13 minutes.

- Allow to cool.

- When cookies are cool, place white chocolate in microwave-safe bowl.

- Microwave twenty seconds at full power and then stir.

- Repeat until chocolate is "mostly" melted and stir. Be careful! It's easy to burn chocolate.

- Dip just the cuff of the mitten in the white chocolate and place on the parchment paper.

- Before chocolate dries, lightly sprinkle with white sanding sugar.

- Place in the fridge for a few minutes to set the chocolate.

- Enjoy!

AFTERWORD

Thanks so much for reading Melinda and Liam's story. I hope their journey made your heart smile. If you did enjoy the book, please consider...

-   Help spreading the word about A Seaside Bookshop Christmas by writing a review.
-   Subscribe to my newsletter in order to receive information about my next release as well as find out about giveaways and special sales.
-   You can like my author page on Facebook or follow me on Twitter.

I hope you'll come back to Bluestar Island and read the continuing adventures of its residents. In upcoming books, there will be updates on Hannah and Ethan as well as the addition of some new islanders.

Coming next is Lainey & Jack's story in A Lighthouse Snapshot.

Thanks again for your support! It is HUGELY appreciated.

Happy reading,
Jennifer

About Author

Award-winning author, Jennifer Faye pens fun, heartwarming contemporary romances. With more than a million books sold, she is internationally published with books translated into more than a dozen languages and her work has been optioned for film. She is a two-time winner of the RT Book Reviews Reviewers' Choice Award, the CataRomance Reviewers' Choice Award, named a TOP PICK author, and been nominated for numerous other awards.

Now living her dream, she resides with her very patient husband and two spoiled cats. When she's not plotting out her next romance, you can find her curled up with a mug of tea and a book. You can learn more about Jennifer at www.JenniferFaye.com

Subscribe to Jennifer's newsletter for news about upcoming releases, bonus content and other special offers.

You can also join her on Twitter, Facebook, or Goodreads.

Made in the USA
Las Vegas, NV
15 January 2024

84412535R00148